PIONEER LOVES

PIONEER LOVES

Ernest Haycox

Thorndike Press • **Chivers Press**
Thorndike, Maine USA **Bath, England**

This Large Print edition is published by Thorndike Press, USA and by Chivers Press, England.

Published in 1997 in the U.S. by arrangement with Golden West Literary Agency.

Published in 1997 in the U.K. by arrangement with Golden West Literary Agency.

U.S.   Hardcover   0-7862-1078-8 (Western Series Edition)
U.K.   Hardcover   0-7540-3016-4 (Chivers Large Print)
U.K.   Softcover   0-7540-3017-2 (Camden Large Print)

Thorndike Large Print ® Western Series.

The text of this Large Print edition is unabridged.
Other aspects of the book may vary from the original edition.

Set in 16 pt. Plantin by Minnie B. Raven.

Printed in the United States on permanent paper.

British Library Cataloguing in Publication Data available

Library of Congress Cataloging in Publication Data

Haycox, Ernest, 1899–1950.
    Pioneer loves / Ernest Haycox.
        p.   cm.
    ISBN 0-7862-1078-8 (lg. print : hc)
    1. Frontier and pioneer life — West (U.S.) — Fiction.
2. Love stories, American.   3. Western stories.
4. Large type books.   I. Title.
[PS3515.A9327P56   1997]
813'.52—dc21   97-331

Contents

Call This Land Home

One at a time, the emigrant families fell out where the land most pleased them, and at last only two wagons of the overland caravan moved southward along the great green valley of Oregon; then the Potters discovered their fair place and John Mercy drove on with his lone wagon, his wife in unhappy silence beside him, and Caroline and young Tom under the canvas cover behind. Through the puckered opening at the wagon's rear young Tom saw the Potters grow dim in the steaming haze of this wet day. Rain lightly drummed on the canvas; he listened to the talk of his people.

"Have we got to live so far from everybody?" his mother asked.

In his father's voice was that fixed mildness which young Tom knew so well. "The heart of a valley's always better than foot or head. I want two things — the falls of a creek for my mill and plenty of open land roundabout."

She said, "Rough riding won't do for me much longer."

"I know," he said, and drove on.

7

In middle afternoon two days later, the wagon stopped and his father said, "I believe we're here." Crawling over the tail gate, young Tom — Thomas Jackson Mercy, age eight — saw the place on which he was to spend the rest of his long life. In three directions the fall-cast green earth ran away in gentle meadow vistas, here and there interrupted by low knobs and little islands of timber, and cross-hatched by the brushy willow borders of creeks. On the fourth side a hill covered by fir and cedar ran down upon the wagon. A stream smaller than a river but bigger than a branch came across the meadows, dropped over a two-foot rock ledge like a bent sheet of glittering glass, and sharply curved to avoid the foot of the hill, running on toward some larger stream beyond view.

John Mercy turned toward the wagon to give his wife a hand, and young Tom noted that she came down with a careful awkwardness. Then his father stamped the spongy earth with his feet and bent over and plunged his tough fingers into the soil and brought up a sample, squeezing and crumbling it and considering it closely. He was a very tall man, a very powerful man, and all his motions were governed by a willful regularity. A short curly beard covered his face as far as the cheekbones; a big nose, scarred white at the bridge, stood over a mouth held firm by constant habit. He seemed to be smiling, but it was less a smile than a moment of keen interest which forced little creases around mouth and eyes. To young Tom, his father, at twenty-eight, was an old man.

John Mercy said, "It will take a week of clear weather to dry this ground for plowing." He turned, looking at the timber close by, and at the rising slope of the hill; he put his hands on his hips, and young Tom knew his father was searching out a place for the cabin. A moment later Mercy swung to face his wife with a slightly changed expression. She had not moved since leaving the wagon; she stood round-shouldered and dejected in the soft rain, reflecting on her face the effect of the gray day, the dampness and the emptiness which lay all around them. Young Tom had never seen her so long idle, for she was brisk in everything she did, always moving from chore to chore.

Mercy said, "In another two years you'll see neighbors wherever you look."

"That's not now," she said.

"The Willamette's beyond this hill somewhere. There's settlers on it."

She said, "I long for back home," and turned from him and stood still again, facing the blind distance.

John Mercy stepped to the wagon and lifted the ax from its bracket. He said to young Tom, "Go cut a small saplin' for a pole, and some uprights," and handed over the ax. Then he got into the wagon and swung it around to drive it under the trees. When young Tom came out of the deeper timber with his saplings, the oxen were un-yoked and a fire burned beneath the massive spread of a cedar. The tail gate was down and his father had reversed an empty tub to make a step from wagon to ground. Between them, they made a frame for the extra tarpaulin to rest on, thereby creating a shelter. His mother stood by, still with her unusual helplessness on her and he knew, from his father's silence, that there was trouble between them.

His father said, "Water, Tom," and went on working. When Tom came back with the big camp kettle filled, his father had driven uprights at either side of the fire, connected by a cross-piece on which the hook hung. He lifted the camp kettle to the hook and listened a moment to the fire hissing against the kettle's wet bottom. The grub box was let down from the wagon box, but his mother was idle at the fire, one arm around Caroline, who stood by her. His father was at the edge of the timber, facing the meadow; he went over.

"Now, then," his father said, "it's sickly weather and we've got to get up a cabin. It'll go here. We'll cut the small trees yonder, for that's where the good house will stand some-day. So we'll be doing two things at the same time — making the cabin and clearing the yard." His eyes, gray to their bottom-most depths, swung around, and their effect was like heavy weight on young Tom. It was seldom that he gave young Tom his undi-vided attention. "We've got everything to do here, and nothing to do it with but our hands. Never waste a lick, and make every lick work twice for you if you can. No man lives long enough to get done all he wants to do, but if he works slipshod and has got to do it over, then he wastes his life. I'll start on that tree. You trim and cut."

The blows of the ax went through the woods in dull echoing, not hurried — for his father never hurried — but with the even tempo of a clock's ticking. His mother worked around the grub box with her dis-heartened slowness. First shadows were sooty in the timber and mist moved in from the meadows. He listened to the sounds of the empty land with fascination; he watched the corridors of the timber for moving

11

things, and he waited for the tree to fall.

The rains quit. Warmed by a mild winter sun, the meadows exhaled fleecy wisps of steam which in young Tom's imagination became the smoke of underground fires breaking through. They dropped trees of matched size, cut and notched and fitted them. When the walls were waist high, Mercy rigged an incline and a block and tackle, but even with that aid his body took the weight of each log, his boots sank deep into the spongy soil and his teeth showed in white flashes when hard effort pulled back his lips.

After supper, with a fire blazing by the cabin, Mercy adzed out the rough boards for window and doorframe and inner furniture, and late at night young Tom woke to hear his father's froe and mallet splitting the cedar roof shakes, and sometimes heard his mother fretfully calling, "Mercy, come now! It's late enough!" Lying awake, he listened to his father come into the wagon and settle down upon the mattress with a groaning sigh and fall at once asleep. The dying yellow of the firelight flickered against the wagon canvas; strange sounds rustled in the windy woods, and far off was the baying of timber wolves. Caroline, disturbed by that wild sound, stirred against him.

The rains held off and the meadows dried before the roof of the cabin was on. John Mercy said, "It might be the last clear spell all winter. I have got to stop the cabin and break that meadow and get the wheat in." He looked at his wife. "Maybe you won't mind living in the wagon a week longer."

"I mind nothing," she said, "except being here."

John Mercy turned to his son. "Go round up the animals."

The two brindled oxen were deep in the meadow. Driving them back to the cabin, Tom saw his people at the campfire; they were saying things not meant for him, his mother with her arms tight across her breasts and her head flung up. Presently his father turned away to yoke the oxen, hitch on the breaking plow and go into the meadow.

The ancient turf became coiled, gloss-brown strips. John Mercy watched the sky as he plowed and worked until the furrows grew ragged in the fading day; and ate and built his fire and hewed out the cabin rafters, and by morning's first twilight shadows he was at work again, harrowing the meadow into rough clods, into pebbled smoothness. The gray clouds thickened in the southwest and the wind broke and whirled them on. With the wheat sack strapped before him like an apron, John Mercy sowed his grain, reaching for the seed, casting with an even sweep, pacing on, and reaching and casting again. Young Tom sawed out the top logs, shortening and angling each cut meant for the cabin's peak; and at night, by the bonfire's swaying glow, he laid his weight against the block-and-tackle rope while his father heaved the logs up the incline into place.

On Sunday his father said, "Take the gun, Tom, and go over this hill and keep on till you find the Willamette. See what you can see. Come back around the side of the hill and tell me which is the short way."

Within a hundred yards the cabin vanished behind the great bark-ribbed firs whose trunks were thicker through than the new cabin. They ran far to the sky and an easy cry came out of them as they swayed to the wind. Pearly shafts of light slanted into this fragrant wilderness place, like the shafts of judgment light shining from heaven to earth in Redway's old geography book. Fern and hazel stood head high to him, and giant deadfalls lay with their red-brown rotted wood crumbling away.

He climbed steadily, now and then crossing short ravines in whose black marsh bottom the devil stock stiffly grew, and stung him as he passed; and down a long vista he saw a buck deer poised alertly at a pool. His gun rose, but then he remembered the cool voice of his father saying, "Never kill meat far from home," and he slapped his hand against the gun stalk and watched the deer go bounding into the deeper forest gloom.

A long two miles brought him to the crest of the hill, from which he saw the surface of a big river showing between the lower trees. Another half mile, very rough, brought him down to the river's margin; he turned to the right and presently the timber and the hill rolled out into the meadowlands. Directly over the river he saw a cabin in a clearing, and saw a girl at the break of the bluff watching him. He looked at her and suffered his short shock of disappointment to find a house and people here, for he had been until this moment a lone explorer pushing through a wild and empty place.

At such a distance he would not clearly see her face; she was about his size, and she stared at him with a motionless interest. He stirred his feet in the soft earth and he raised his hand and waved it, but she continued to look at him, not answering, and in a little while he turned and followed the open meadows as they bent around the toe of the dark hill and reached home before noon.

His father said, "What did you see?"

"The river's on the other side of the hill, but it's easier to go around the hill. I saw a deer."

"That's all?"

"And a cabin across the river," said Tom. "There was a girl in the yard."

John Mercy looked to his wife. "Now," he said quietly, "there's one neighbor," and waited for her answer.

She looked at him, reluctant to be pleased. "How far away?"

Young Tom said, "More than an hour, I guess."

His mother said, "If they saw you, they'll come to visit . . . and it's a terrible camp they'll see . . . Caroline, go scrub and change your dress. I've got to fix your hair." Suddenly she was irritably energetic, moving around to put away the scattered pans and the loose things lying under the canvas shelter.

John Mercy went toward a pile of saplings roughly cut into rafters; he cast a secret glance of benevolence at young Tom. Something had pleased him. He said, "We'll get these on in short order."

The saplings went up and crosspoles were set across them. The first row of shakes was laid when a man's strong halloo came ringing in from the meadow and a family moved through the trees, man and wife, two tall boys carrying sacks, and the girl young Tom noticed across the river.

The man said in a great, grumbling voice, "Neighbor, by the Lord, we could of saved you sweat on that cabin if we'd known you were here. Teal is my name. Iowa."

Talk broke through this quiet like a sudden storm. The two women moved beyond the wagon, and young Tom heard their voices rush back and forth in tumbling eagerness. The men were at the cabin.

Teal said, "Boys, you're idle. This man needs shakes for his roof. Go split 'em. It's a-going to rain, Mercy, and when it rains here, it's the world drowned out. The drops are big as banty eggs. They bust like ripe watermelons, they splatter, they splash. You're soaked, your shoes squash, you steam like a kettle on a fire. Boys, don't stand there. Mercy and me will lay on what shakes that's cut."

The Teal girl stood in front of young Tom and stared at him with direct curiosity. She was not quite his height; she was berry brown, with small freckles on her nose, and her hair hung down behind in one single braid. Caroline cautiously moved forward and looked to the Teal girl, and suddenly

17

put out a hand and touched her dress. The Teal girl took Caroline's hand, but she kept her eyes on young Tom.

"I saw you," she said.

"What's your name?"

"Mary," said the Teal girl, and turned with the quickest motion and walked toward the older women.

The Teal boys worked on shakes, one splitting, one drawing the cedar panels down with the knife. The wind lifted and the roar of it was the dashing of giant cataracts all through the deep places in the forest; the men talked steadily as they worked. The smell of frying steak — brought by the Teals — was in the air to tantalize young Tom. He leaned against a tree and watched Mary Teal from the corner of his eye, then turned and walked away from the trees to the falls of the creek and squatted at the edge of the pool, his shadow sending the loafing trout into violent crisscross flight. Gray clouds ran low over the land and a deepening haze crawled forward. He hunched himself together, like a savage over a fire; he listened into the wind and waited for the scurrying shapes of the enemy to come trotting in war file out of the misty willow clumps. He sat there a long while, the day dull around him. The wind increased and the pool's silver surface showed the pocking of rain. His mother's voice called him back to mealtime.

He ate by the fire, listening to the voices of the older people go on and on. His mother's face was red from the heat of the fire, and her eyes were bright and she was smiling; his father sat comfortably under the cedar tree, thawed by the company. It was suddenly half dark, the rain increasing, and the Teals rose and spoke their farewells and filed off through the trees, Mr. Teal's last cheerful call returning to them.

Silence returned; loneliness deepened.

His mother said, "It was good to see people."

"They'll be fine neighbors," his father said.

His mother's face tightened. She looked over the flames and suddenly seemed to remember her fears. "Four miles away," she said, and turned to the dishes on the camp table. She grew brisk. "Tom, I want water. Stack these dishes, Caroline, and come out of the rain."

John Mercy went into the darkness beyond the cabin and built his work fire; lying awake in bed, young Tom heard his father's mallet steadily splitting out shakes, and he continued to hear the sound in his sleep.

★ ★ ★

By morning a great wind cried across the world. John Mercy lighted the campfire and cooked breakfast for the women within the wagon. He laid on heavy logs for the fire's long burning and took a piece of rope and the ax and hammer and nails. "We have got a chore to do at the river," he said to young Tom. "You pack the gun." They skirted the foot of the hill, trailing beside a creek stained muddy by the storm. The meadow turf was spongy underfoot and the southwest wind roughly shoved them forward through sheets of fat raindrops sparkling in the mealy light. When they reached the river they saw a lamp burning in the window of the Teal house, but John Mercy swung to a place where the hill's timber met the bluff of the stream.

"There will come a time," he said, "when I'll have to send you to the Teals' for help. You'll need a raft to cross."

They cut down and trimmed six saplings for a raft bed, bound them with two cross-pieces nailed in. A pole, chipped flat at one end, made an oar. Then John Mercy tied the rope to the raft and towed it upstream a hundred yards beyond the Teal house. He drew it half from the water and secured the rope to an overhanging tree and laid the oar in the brush. "You'll drift as you paddle," he said.

Homeward-bound, the wind came at them face on. Young Tom bent against it, hearing his father's half-shouted words, "It ought to be a month or more before the baby's due. But we're alone out here, and accidents come along. We've got to expect those things. No sensible man watches his feet hit ground. He looks ahead to see what kind of ground they'll hit next."

They came around a bend of the creek and heard a massive cannon crack of sound in the hills above them, and the ripping fall of a tree; its jarring collision with the earth ran out to them. They pressed on, John Mercy's pace quickening as though a new thought disturbed him. High in the air was an echo like the crying of a bird, lasting only a moment and afterward shredded apart by the storm, but it rose again thinner and wilder and became a woman's voice screaming.

John Mercy's body broke from its chanthe neled steadiness and he rushed around the last bend of the hill, past the pool of the falls and into the cabin clearing. Young Tom followed, the gun across his chest. Through the trees he saw a figure by the campfire, not his mother's figure, but a dark head and a dark face standing above some kind of cloak. His father stopped at the fire before the stranger; reaching the scene, young Tom discovered that the stranger was an Indian. His mother stood back against the wagon with a butcher knife in her hand; her face shocked him, white and strange-stretched as it was.

He lifted the gun, waiting. The Indian was old and his cheeks were round holes rimmed by jawbone and temple. His eyes were sick. His hand, stretched through the blanket, was like the foot of a bird, nothing but bone and wrinkled dark flesh. He spoke something, he pointed at the food locker. For a moment — for a time-stopped space in which the acid clarity of this scene ate its way so deeply into young Tom's memory that ninety years of living neither changed nor dimmed a detail of it — he watched the latent danger rise around his father's mouth and flash in his eyes; then, with complete unexpectedness, his father turned to the grub box and found half a loaf of bread. He laid it in the Indian's fingers — those fingers closing down until they almost disappeared in the bread. His father pointed at the gun in young Tom's hand and pointed back to the Indian, snapping down his thumb as though firing; he seized the Indian at the hips, lifting him like a half-emptied sack, walked a few steps and dropped him and gave him an onward push. The Indian went away without looking behind him, his shoulders bent.

His mother's voice, high-pitched and breathless, drew young Tom's attention. She was shaking, and in her eyes was great wildness. "I don't want to be here! I didn't want to come! Mercy, you've got to take me home! I want my old house back! I want my people! I'll die here!"

John Mercy said, "Tom, take your sister for a walk."

Caroline stood in the doorway of the cabin, frightened by the scene. Young Tom went over to catch her hand. The half-covered roof kept Caroline dry, and he stood indecisively under this shelter disliking to leave it, yet compelled by his father's order.

John Mercy lifted his wife into his arms, speaking, "The creature was harmless. There are no bad Indians around here. I know the weather's poor and there's no comfort, but I'll have the roof on the cabin by tonight." He carried her into the wagon, still talking.

Young Tom heard his mother's voice rising again, and his father's patient answering. He clung to Caroline's hand and watched the rain-swept world beyond the cabin and saw no other shelter to which he might go. He was hard pressed to make up his mind, and when his father came out of the wagon, he said in self-defense, "Caroline would get awfully wet if I took her for a walk."

John Mercy said, "You did right. Caroline, go keep your mother company." He looked to the unfinished roof, he drew a hand down across his waster-crusted beard, and for a moment he remained stone-still, his whole body sagged down with its accumulation of weariness. He drew a long breath and straightened. "Soon as I finish the roof, Tom, we'll line the fireplace with clay. I'll need some straw to mix with the clay. You go along the creek where the old hay's rotted down. Bring me several swatches of it."

The rain walked over the earth in constant sheets, beating down grass and weeds and running vines; the creek grew violent between its banks and the increased falls dropped roaring into its pool. Bearing his loads of dead grass to the cabin, young Tom watched his father lay the last rows of shakes on the roof and cap the ridge with boards hewn out earlier by the late firelight; afterward John Mercy, working faster against the fading day, went beside the creek to an undercut bank and shoveled out its clay soil, carrying it back to the cabin by bucket. He cooked a quick supper and returned to the cabin, mixing clay and dead grass stems, and coated the wood fireplace and its chimney with this mortar. He built a small fire, which, by drying the mud, would slowly season it to a brick-hard lining.

Throughout the night, fitfully waking, young Tom heard the dull thumping of a hammer, and twice heard his mother call out, "Mercy, come to bed!" At daybreak young Tom found a canvas door at the cabin; inside, a fire burned on the dirt hearth and a kettle steamed from the crane. The crevices between logs were mud-sealed, the table and grub box and benches had been brought in. Standing before the fire, young Tom heard the wind search the outer wall and fall away, and suddenly the warmth of the place thawed the coldness which lay beneath his skin. He heard his mother come in, and he turned to see his parents standing face to face, almost like strangers.

His mother said, "Mercy, did you sleep at all?"

His father's answer was somehow embarrassed. "I had to keep the fire alive, so the mud would dry right. Today I'll get the puncheons on the floor and we can move the beds in." In a still gentler voice, the uncertainness of apology in it, his father added, "Maybe, if you shut your eyes and think how all this will look five years from now —"

She cut him off with the curt swing of her body, and walked to the fire. Stooping with a slowness so unlike her, she laid the Dutch oven against the flame and went to the grub box. She put her yellow mixing bowl on the table, she got her flour and her shortening and her salt. She stood a moment over the mixing bowl, not looking at John Mercy. "As long as I can do my share, I'll do it. Tom, fetch me the pail of water."

He stood with his father at the break of the trees, viewing the yellow-gray turf of the meadow, and the plowed ground beyond it, and the valley floor running away to the great condensed wall of mist. He knew, from the dead gentleness of tone, that his father was very tired; it was not like him to waste time speaking of the future. "The orchard will go right in front of this spot," his father said. "That will be pretty to look at from the house. The house will stand where we're standing. These firs will go down." He was silent, drawing the future forward and finding comfort in it. "All this is free — all this land. But it's up to a man to make something out of it. So there's nothing free. There never is. We'll earn every acre we get. Don't trust that word 'free.' Don't believe it. You'll never own anything you didn't pay for. But what you pay for is yours. You've got it while other men wait around for something free, and die with nothing. Now, then, we have got to cut down some small firs, about eight inches through. We'll split them in half for floor puncheons."

He turned, walking slower than usual; he searched the trees, nodding at one or the other, and stopped at a thin fir starved by the greater firs around it; its trunk ran twenty feet without a branch. "That one," he said, and went to the cabin wall for his ax. "Tom," he said, "I want you to go up in the hills and see how close you can find a ledge of rock. That's for the fireplace floor." He faced the tree, watching the wind whip its top; he made an undercut on the side toward which he wished the tree to fall, and squared himself away to a steady chopping.

Young Tom passed the cabin, upward bound into the semi-darkness of the hill; the great trees groaned in their swaying, and their shaken branches let down ropy spirals of rain. It was like walking into a tunnel full of sound. His overcoat grew heavy with water which, dripping on his trousers legs, turned them into ice-cold bands; his shoes were mushy. Behind him he heard the first crackling of the tree going down, and he turned and saw his father running. The tree, caught by the wind, was falling the wrong way. He shouted against the wind; his father looked behind, saw the danger and jumped aside. The tree, striking a larger fir, bounced off, and young Tom saw its top branches whip out and strike his father to the ground. His father shouted, buried somewhere beneath that green covering.

His mother came crying out of the cabin. "Mercy! Mercy!" She stumbled and caught herself, and rushed on, fighting the branches away as she reached the tree.

When he got there, he saw his father lying with both legs beneath the trunk. The branches, first striking, had broken the force of the trunk's fall; and then they had shattered, to let the trunk down upon his father who lay on an elbow with his lips the color of gray flour paste. Young Tom never knew until then how piercing a gray his father's eyes were.

His mother cried, "Your legs! Oh, God, Mercy!" She bent over him, she seized the trunk of the tree and she stiffened under her straining. John Mercy's voice was a vast shout of warning, "Martha, don't do that!" His arm reached out and struck her on the hip. "Let go!" She drew back and laid both arms over her stomach, a shock of pain pressing her face into its sharp angles. "Oh, Mercy," she said, "it's too late!" and stared down at him in terror.

Young Tom raced to the cabin wall, got the shovel and rushed back; a branch interfered with his digging. He found the ax, thrown ten yards away by Mercy in his flight; he returned to cut the limb away. Mercy lay still, as though he were listening. He watched his wife, and he put a hand over his eyes and seemed to be thinking; the impact of the ax on the trunk threw twinges of pain through him, but he said nothing until young Tom had finished.

"Give me the shovel," he said. "Now go get Mrs. Teal."

Young Tom stood irresolute. "You got to get out of there."

"Those legs," said John Mercy, and spoke of them as though they didn't belong to him, "are pinched. If they were broken, I'd know it . . . and they're not." He paused and a dead gray curtain of pain came down on his face; he suffered it and waited for it to pass. "Do as I tell you." Young Tom whirled and started away at a hard run, and was almost instantly checked and swung by his father's command, "You've got a long way to go, and you'll not do it starting that fast. Steady now. I've told you before. Think ahead."

Young Tom began again, trotting out upon the meadow; he looked back and saw his father awkwardly working with the shovel, sheltered by the outstretched apron of his mother. But even before young Tom ceased to look, she dropped the apron, put both hands before her face and walked toward the wagon.

The scene frightened him, and he broke into a dead run along the margin of the creek, and began to draw deep into his lungs for wind; he ran with his fists doubled, his arms lunging back and forth across his chest. A pain caught him in the side, and he remembered his father's advice and slowed to a dogtrot. He grew hot and stopped once to crawl down the bank of a creek for a drink, and was soon chilled by the wet ground against his stomach and the rain beating on his back.

After a rest of a minute he went on, stiffened by that short pause. The river willows at last broke through the rain mist forward, and the low shape of the Teal cabin. He crossed the last meadow and came to the bank; he hadn't forgotten the raft, but he wanted to save time. The wind was with him, carrying his shrill call over the water.

He repeated it twice before the cabin door opened and Mrs. Teal stepped to the yard. Young Tom raised his arm, pointing behind him toward his home. Mrs. Teal waved back at him immediately and ran into the house.

Squatted on the bank, young Tom saw the three Teal men come out, lift a boat and carry it to the water; in a moment Mrs. Teal joined them, and the four came over the river. Mrs. Teal had a covered basket in her hand.

She said, "Your mother, Tom?"

"My father's caught under a sapling that fell on him. That made mother sick."

Teal turned on his lank, Indian-dark sons. "Git ahead and help him."

"Oh, Lord, Lord," said Mrs. Teal. "Take the basket, Nate. We've got to go fast. It's going to be unnatural."

Young Tom started after the Teal boys, they running away with a loose and ranging ease. "No," said Teal, "you stay with us. You've had runnin' enough. The boys are a pair of hounds; let 'em go."

They went forward, Mrs. Teal now and then speaking to herself with a soft exclamation of impatience. Otherwise there was no talk. The wind was against them and the rain beat down. Young Tom opened his mouth to let the great drops loosen his dry throat, and silently suffered the slow pace. The coming baby never entered his mind; it was his father lying under the tree that he thought of with dread, and when the creek began to bend around the toe of the hills, close by the falls, he ran ahead and reached the house.

His father had dug himself out from the trap; there was a little tunnel of earth where he had been. The two boys stood silently at the fire, and one of them motioned toward the cabin. Young Tom drew the doorway canvas back from the logs, looking in; his father had moved the bedstead from the wagon and had set it up near the cabin's fireplace. His mother was on it, groaning, and his father knelt at the bedside and held her hands. Young Tom retreated to the fire, watching the Teals come through the trees. Mrs. Teal seized the basket from her husband and went at once into the cabin; a moment later his father came out.

John Mercy said to Teal, "It's a good thing to have neighbors. I'm sorry I can't offer you coffee at this minute." He let his chin drop and he spread his hands before the fire and gravely watched it. The sockets of his eyes seemed deep and blackened; his mouth was a line straight and narrow across his skin.

"My friend," said Teal, "the first winter's

always a bad one. Don't work so hard or you'll be twenty years older by spring."

He turned to the taller of his two sons. "Joe, take Mercy's gun and go fetch in a deer."

Young Tom heard his mother's sharp cry from the cabin. He moved away, he stood by the tree and stared at the trench in which his father had been, and noticed the marks scrubbed into the soft ground by his father's elbows. He walked along the tree and gave it a kick with his foot, and continued to the millpond. Here he squatted, watching the steamy rain mists pack tight along the willows of the creek. In the distance, a mile or so, a little timbered butte stood half concealed by the fog, seeming to ride free in the low sky. He tightened his muscles, waiting for the enemy to come single file through the brush, but then he thought of the old savage, so bony and stooped and unclean, who had seized the half loaf of bread, and his picture of a row of glistening copper giants was destroyed. He heard voices by the cabin, and rose and saw Mrs. Teal by the fire. He went back.

Mrs. Teal looked at him with her kindness. "Your mother's all right, Tom. You had a brother, but he wasn't meant to stay. You understand, Tom? It's meant that way and you oughtn't sorrow."

She meant the baby boy was dead. He thought about it and wanted to feel like crying, but he hadn't seen this boy and he didn't know anything about him, and didn't know what to cry for. It embarrassed him not to feel sad. He stood with his eyes on the fire.

Teal said to his other son, "That Methodist preacher is probably down at Mission Bottom, Pete. You go home, get the horse and go for him." He walked a little distance onward, speaking in a lower tone to his son. Then the son went on, and Teal turned back to the cabin and got the saw standing by the wall and went over to the fallen log. He called to young Tom, "Now then, let's not be idle men. Puncheons he wanted, wasn't it? We'll just get 'em ready while we wait."

A shot sounded deeper in the forest — one and no more, "There's your meat," said Teal. "You've seen the trout in the creek, ain't you? Mighty fat. Next summer there'll be quail all through those meadow thickets. What you've got to have is a horse for ridin'. Just a plain ten-dollar horse. I know where there's one."

The minister arrived around noon the next day, and out of this wet and empty land the neighbors began to come, riding or walking in from all quarters of the mist-hidden valley, destroying forever young Tom's illusion of wilderness. They came from the scattered claims along the river, from French Prairie, from the upper part of the La Creole, from strangely named creeks and valleys as far as twenty miles away; the yard was filled with men, and women worked in the cabin and at the fire outside the cabin. Young Tom stared at strange boys running through the timber, and resented their trespassing; he heard girls giggling in the shelter of the wagon. It was a big meeting. A heavy man in buckskins, light of eye and powerfully voiced, strolled through the crowd and had a word for everyone. People visited and the talk was of the days of the wagon-train crossing, of land here and land there, of politics and the Hudson's Bay Company. A group of men walked along the break of the hill until they reached a knoll a hundred yards from the cabin. He watched them digging.

In a little while they returned, bringing quietness to the people. The minister came from the cabin, bareheaded in the rain. Mr. Teal followed, carrying a small bundle wrapped within a sheet and covered by a shawl; they went on toward the grave, and young Tom, every sense sharpened, heard the knocking of a hammer and the calling of a voice. The crowd moved over and his father walked from the cabin, carrying his mother. Young Tom saw Caroline alone at the cabin's doorway, crying; he went to her and got her hand and followed his father.

A little box stood at the grave, the minister by it; he had a book in his hand which he watched while the rain dripped down his long face. Young Tom's mother was on her feet, but she wasn't crying, though all the women around her were. The minister spoke a long while, it seemed to Tom. He held Caroline's hand and grew cold, waiting for the minister's words to end. Somebody said, "Amen," and the minister began a song, all the people joining.

Looking at his feet, young Tom felt the coldness run up his legs, and his chest was heavy and he, too, cried. As soon as the song was done, his father carried his mother back to the house and the crowd returned to the fire. A woman dumped venison steaks into a big kettle on the table, and cups and plates went around and the talk grew brisker than it had been before,

Young Tom said, "Caroline, you go into the wagon." From the corners of his eyes he saw men shoveling dirt into the grave;

he thought about the grave and imagined the rains filling it with water, and the shawl and the white sheet growing black in the mud. He went over to the fallen log and sat on it.

He remained there, wholly lost in the forest of his imagination while the round-about neighbors, finished with eating and finished with visiting, started homeward through the dulling day. They went in scattered groups, as they had come, their strong calling running back and forth in the windy rain; and at last only the Teals remained. He saw Caroline and Mary Teal watching him through the front opening of the wagon. He rose and went around to the cabin, hearing the older Teals talking.

Mrs. Teal said, "I'm needed. We'll stay tonight."

Teal looked at his two tall sons. "You had best get at those puncheons. Mercy's legs will trouble him for a while. Tomorrow we are agoin' to knock down some trees for a barn lean-to."

Young Tom quietly drew back the canvas covering of the cabin's doorway. He was troubled about his mother and wanted to see her, and meant to go in. But what he saw suddenly shut him out and brought great embarrassment to him.

His father stood beside the bed, looking down, and young Tom heard him say, "I can't stay here when your heart's not in it. There is no pleasure in this work, and no point in looking ahead to what it'll be some-day, if you don't feel it too. Well, you don't. We'll go home in the spring when it's possible to travel. That's what you want, I clearly know."

She was pale and her eyes were stretched perfectly round; her head rolled slightly, her voice was very small. "I couldn't leave now. I've got a baby buried here. It's a mighty hard way to come to love a country . . . to lose something in it. Mercy, put a railing round that grave. I have not been of much use, I know, and it's hurt me to see you work the way you've done. It will be better when I can get up and do what I can do."

John Mercy bent down and kissed his wife, and suddenly in young Tom the embarrassment became intolerable, for this was a thing he had never seen his people do before, and a thing he was to see again only twice so long as they lived. He pulled back and let the canvas fall into place; he thought he heard his father crying. He walked by the big kettle with its remaining chunks of fried venison steak. He took one, eating it like a piece of bread. Caroline and Mary Teal were now at the back end of the wagon, looking at him.

He said, "I know a big cave up on the hill."

Mary Teal came from the wagon, Caroline following; and the three walked into the woods, into the great sea swells of sound poured out by the rolling timber crowns. Mary gave him a sharp sidewise glance and smiled, destroying the strangeness between them and giving him a mighty feeling of comfort. The long, long years were beginning for Tom Mercy, and he was to see that smile so many times again in the course of his life, to be warmed and drawn on by it, to see tears shining through it, and broken thoughts hidden by it. To the last day of his life far out in another century, that smile — real or long after remembered — was his star, but like a star, there was a greater heat within it than he was ever to feel or to know.

No Time for Dreams

Katherine turned the wheat out of the lye water, washed it carefully six times, and poured it into the iron kettle over the fire; that was supper — the entire supper. A woolly November rain rolled through the giant firs around her and crusted her cloak with its sparkling beads as she ran toward her wagon. She paused a moment to call up to the Rowley wagon, inside which Mrs. Rowley lay sick with a cold.

"Ella, the wheat's on to boil! I'll watch! Don't get up!"

She climbed the high seat of her own wagon and got beneath the shelter of the canvas stretched over its bows. This was her home, and had been since leaving Independence, Missouri, five months and twenty-three days before. Her mattress and comforters lay in a corner opposite her mother's lowboy; everything else — the trunks and boxes, the dishes in their barrels, the farm tools, the seedling fruit switches bedded in dirt boxes — were closely packed around her. She got out her father's writing box, lighted a candle, and went on with the letter she had been composing for so long a time for her married sister in the East:

. . . Everything went well until we got to the crossing of the Platte. Then cholera came. Mother took it first, father next. George and Saul died last. They're buried not far from the river, but you and I will never find their graves. The Rowleys were kind — they took me in. We kept the wagon, and a young man in the party helped me with the oxen. His name is Ben McLane and he reminds me of Saul. He's that tall and has red hair almost like Saul's.

We're camped in the trees behind Portland village. Half the train turned off at Fort Hall for California. Most of the rest went south from Oregon City into the Willamette. We're just ten wagons left. The men are all out in a valley beyond here to see what land can be had. I don't know what I'll do yet. The Rowleys are poor and I'm one more mouth to feed. There's not six dollars in all ten families. Maybe you think I ought to feel sadder than I sound. Well, I have cried, but out here you can't cry long. Maybe someday when other things are done, I'll cry again.

The men were returning, riding or walking the thick mud trail through the trees toward the wagons parked in the forest gloom. Ben McLane went on to the fire and crouched down against it. She watched him through the round opening of the wagon canvas with an attention so complete that it left no room for anything else in her mind; and presently she climbed from the wagon and went over to the fire to stir the wheat in the kettle. He looked up to her. The long ride in the rain had chilled him and he seemed low of spirits. He was a tall boy with big hands and long arms and a smooth, usually cheerful face.

"Land in the Tualatin's all taken up," he said. "We've decided to go down the valley a hundred miles or so. They say it's open there." His hair rolled back around his temples for want of trimming and his lids crept together as he looked back into the fire. He spread his hands to soak in the heat; steam rolled from his shirt.

Other fires were springing up through the shadows as these families made their supper. She laid her hands quietly together, remembering the things she and Ben had talked about on the long ride across the desert, and she searched her mind for some single hint that he thought about her as she thought about him. Nothing came out of her memory. He was a quiet man, and she was quiet, too, and had no way of making him see.

A sudden impulse gave her courage for a moment, and she decided she would smile at him in a warmer way. She would push herself that far because it was important, because time grew short and she couldn't live on hope forever. In a little while the silence caused him to look up to her, and she gave him the smile, inwardly praying he would be interested; he watched her a moment, not seeing what was in her mind, and by that she knew he had no great interest in her. She turned back to the wagon and laid the writing box across her lap. She had known it would end this way; her hope had been foolish.

The men have come back and the wagons will go south in the morning. I shall not go. The Rowleys are too poor, and I have been on their kindness long enough. I talked to a woman in the village today. Her husband runs the store and she boards single men. I think I can work there. It is a hard thing to part with people. I shall never see any of them any more.

It is such a lonely world tonight.

She sealed the letter, addressed it, and left the wagon with her cloak drawn around her. A few men had come to the Rowley fire to join Rowley and Ben McLane.

As she went by them, Rowley said, "Where you goin', Katherine?"

"To the store," she said.

Ben McLane's glance came over to her, and for a moment she thought he might rise and walk with her. She looked at him until she knew she could no longer let the moment drag on, and turned away, following the trail through the woods to the village with its two dozen houses scattered beside the big river.

Spicer's store was a long building of squared logs in whose windows a yellow light glowed against the wholly dark night. The sudden fragrance of supper came upon her when she stepped inside. A great whale-oil lamp hung over a serious man who was working out some last-minute account in his ledger; he looked up at her and murmured, "Wife's in the kitchen and wants to see you," and returned to his calculations.

She walked to the kitchen door and found Mrs. Spicer turning a pan of biscuits onto a plate. Mrs. Spicer was a tall, tired, once-pretty woman with a mouth pressed together.

"You're back," she said to Katherine. "You've decided on it?"

"I'll be here as soon as the wagons leave in the morning."

Mrs. Spicer said, "If I take you, will you promise to stay a year?"

Katherine gave the question serious thought. If she made a promise, it had to be kept. The biscuits meanwhile were growing cold; she picked up the plate and carried it to the dining room — to the bachelors' table of young men making their way in this settlement — and laid the biscuits before a blond lad at the table's foot. The blond lad looked at her with his quiet interest, and a liveliness came upon the nine other young men. She turned back to the kitchen.

"Yes, I'll stay," she said to Mrs. Spicer. "I'll come in the morning."

She returned through the weeping woods to find the men all gathered around the Rowley fire for a talk. She went to the Rowley wagon and got into it to tell Mrs. Rowley. Mrs. Rowley said, "Oh, Katherine, what'll we do without you?" But somewhere on this woman's kind face was a fleeting bit of relief; to Mrs. Rowley it meant one less mouth to feed. Going to her own wagon, Katherine got into bed and lay long awake;

dampness made the blankets sticky, and dampness was a powdered wetness in the air around her. Hope was hard to kill, for even though she knew it was foolish, she tried to frame a last message that would reach out to Ben McLane. Long afterwards she fell asleep.

She rose at the first sound of men shouting at the oxen in the darkness. The wagons were hitched, breakfast was eaten and the children stowed away. Mrs. Rowley hugged her, climbed to the seat and burst into tears. Standing by the fire, Katherine watched the big cumbersome wagons swing into line and slowly roll away. She waved at the Rowleys, but she had her eyes on Ben McLane, who rode beside the column on his horse. His good-by to her had been a few words quietly spoken. She watched his tall body fade into the forest gloom and she pressed her mouth together, and a bitter loneliness came to her, and she tried to memorize how he looked before he faded from her sight; for she had liked him and would have married him, and now would see him no more. As soon as the caravan disappeared, she went to her own wagon and drove to the village.

She sold the oxen and the wagon, stored the family goods in an empty log house at the edge of the village; heeled the seedling trees into a sandy patch hard by the river. Mrs. Spicer wondered why Katherine should take the trouble to do this; in Mrs. Spicer's hardwork life, time was precious and not to be spent on unnecessary things.

"No," said Katherine, "I mean to plant them someday on a place of my own, and when they grow up, I'll think of my people."

"It's a hard thing to lose your people," said Mrs. Spicer.

"Hard things happen," said Katherine.

Two days after Katherine came, Mrs. Spicer took to her bed, at last able to afford the luxury of being sick. Katherine rose at five, combed her hair in the cold corner room, lighted the fires and got the breakfast for the boarders. She did the housework in the gray forenoons, planned dinner and cooked and served it. Around two o'clock she had an hour for herself and, with her sewing, she kept Mrs. Spicer company; at four she was again in the kitchen, making up supper. She washed, she baked, she scrubbed the puncheon floors, which grew so dirty from the muddy feet of men. She mended Spicer's shirts, she darned socks for Abbott Corning, who was Spicer's clerk — that blond young man she had noticed at the foot of the table on her first day. All days were long and it was never much before eleven when she closed the door of her room, braided up her hair and lay a moment wide-awake, to think of all that had happened, to remember her people, and to bring close to her the image of Ben McLane. She heard his voice, she saw him on the big wagon beside her and she saw his broad back fading away through the trees, and always at that point the room was a silent, lonely place and sadness lay as a lump within her.

Mrs. Spicer, catching up on her rest, at last had time to consider other people, and spoke to Katherine. "You needn't work so hard. Don't be a drudge like me. Anyhow, I'll be up pretty soon."

Katherine showed Mrs. Spicer a smile. "I'd not hurry. Let your men miss you a while longer."

"They do take things for granted," said Mrs. Spicer. . . . "Katherine, what's ahead for you? What's in your busy mind?"

"Oh, I'll get married."

"It won't be hard to do," said Mrs. Spicer dryly. "The country's full of men. I could name six now that will be askin' you sooner or later. You've got your choice."

Katherine looked away from Mrs. Spicer, out through the window into the steady mists of winter's rain. Her face took on its expression of wonder. "It's not the wanting of many men that counts," she said. "It's the one man who doesn't want."

"Was there a man in that wagon train?"

"Yes," said Katherine.

"What was he like?"

"He's big and red-haired, like my brother Saul. Ben's his name. He'll be a farmer somewhere."

"Nothing was said between you?"

"Oh, no."

Mrs. Spicer looked directly at the ceiling. Her glance went through it, away from this village to a place far off from here and to a time in the past. "Katherine," she murmured, "there've been a lot of women with Bens to remember." She soon brought herself back, her face resuming its fretful impatience. "But you've certainly got your choice now."

She certainly had, for all the young men at the table were single and had venturesome eyes. They were foot-loose ones who had crossed the plains or jumped the sailing ships which touched here. Four were woodcutters, three were hunters, one was a surveyor, one a pony-express messenger, and one was Abbott Corning. He was the quietest of the lot, and the one who already had found his opening. He had begun a log house across from Spicer's and worked on it after hours; it was to be his own store.

"I have got a consignment of goods coming around the Horn on the *Sea Witch* next spring," he told Katherine.

"Won't you be trading against Mr. Spicer?"

"No, he's general merchandise, and I'll be hardware."

He, least of the young group, seemed to want to catch her attention; yet it was he who walked with her on a clear Sunday to the log house at the edge of the settlement and helped her unpack the trunks and air out her people's things. He was from Massachusetts, with a bit of twang in his voice and an agreeable coolness of manner. He was methodical, he was courteous — and now and then she noticed a far-off shining of repressed humor in his eyes.

When they were finished with the airing he strolled toward the river with her to have a look at the heeled-in fruit whips. He put his hands behind his back while he studied the plants; then he looked up at her, and she saw that he had been touched.

"You've not had it easy. We're a long way from home and it's not good to be alone.

Those would make a nice orchard behind a house. What's your last name, Katherine?"

"Millison."

He had taken off his hat, either as a deliberate thing or as an unconscious gesture. It gave her a moment of warmth — it was an understanding he seemed to share with her.

That same feeling came again a little later when he opened a twenty-pound mat of rough sugar from the Sandwich Islands and found a colony of mice living within. He was on the point of throwing the sugar away, but she took it and boiled it out in a kettle and made it into sirup. "Now," he said, "that's practical." In the morning when she served some of the sirup with hot cakes, he grinned at her and nodded toward the other men at the table. "They don't know how good this is, do they?" The understanding moved between them again with its nice feeling.

Mrs. Spicer noticed it, and watched the two through the days, and was thoughtful and more than usually short with her husband. She said nothing to Katherine until she found the girl standing at the store's doorway, looking toward the hills.

"Katherine," she said, "you got a hope maybe Ben will come back?"

"I guess I have," said the girl. "It's a foolish thing."

"He ever know you had him on your mind?"

"Oh, no," said Katherine. "I never showed it." She shrugged her shoulders. "It's just a thing I can't have. People have got to make the best of what comes."

"You're a firm girl," said Mrs. Spicer. She stood beside Katherine, staring at the homely village and its street of churned mud and its gloomy forest crowding down. A sudden dead hatred came to her face. "Sometimes it's almost too much."

Winter settled over the two dozen houses of the village. The hard rains slashed down, turning the street into a quagmire, and the sun came out and steam rose from the forest as though it were afire. These dark evenings Abbott Corning planed out his boards and built his shelves and his counters and sealed in the back room, which was to be living quarters. Seldom did he quit before midnight and, remembering the raw chill of that empty building, Katherine got in the habit of taking coffee to him.

Sometimes, when he put aside his hammer, his weariness made him appear old, but another time, on the day the building was finished, she saw a different side. The young bachelors chose to christen the place with the blue ruin which sold along the river at two dollars the gallon. She was in the kitchen, long past midnight, when he came into Spicer's. He walked down the store aisle with an exaggerated care and halted in the kitchen's doorway. His beaver hat sat angled on his bright blond hair and his eyes were young and sparking with venture. He removed his hat and made his bow, and he looked at her in the way that was new, and strong with personal interest.

"Katherine," he said, "I have got a store. There's nothing in it yet, but I have got it. I'm not a fool often, but I get to thinking sometimes the fools have the best of it. Every board I planed and cut and doweled down, every board came out of time I could have been sleeping or fishing on the river. I thought I'd be a fool for once. Have I done wrong?" He was laughing as he said it, but he was anxious about it, too, and watched her pour coffee for him, and took the cup obediently.

"It's nice to be free once in a while," she said. "I'm glad you did. You drink that and you'll not feel bad tomorrow."

He drank it and smiled at her. "You ought not be so troubled, Katherine, and I ought not be so dull."

"I'll laugh someday, like you're laughing now," she said. "And you're not dull at all." She took him by the arm and led him over the store to his room.

He stood by his bed with the strong admiration in his eyes, but even then she knew she had nothing to fear from him. She gave him a small push. He fell back on the bed and he lay there, his hair tousled and his eyes closed. "It's been satisfactory," he murmured. "I'll never be an old man with a skullcap and muttonchop whiskers."

On the third of April, the bark *Sea Witch* worked up the river to tie at the bluff with Abbott Corning's consignment of goods from Boston. He hired the bachelors to move the cargo into his store, and on another night, a week later, he brought a sign out of a hiding place — a white shingle blackly lettered: CORNING & CO. HARDWARE, TIN GOODS, CROCKERY, MINERS' SUPPLIES, LEATHER. He went into the dark street and hung it to the waiting bracket over the doorway and came back. A rainy wind rushed over the town and the shingle began to squeak in its metal eyes. He put his hands into his trousers pockets and stood before her. He was quiet, he was happy.

"I shall open this door in the morning. I hope to open it, the same key in the same lock, as long as I'm alive." He jingled the coins in his pocket, he smiled, he settled his shoulders. "I am twenty-three years old and I owe twenty thousand dollars on this stock. My health is good. I am ambitious. I can be trusted. I am not a lively man." The smiling dissolved into great seriousness. "I would be happy if you saw fit to trust me, as others have done . . . if you'd make the venture with me . . . if you'd be my wife."

She had one terrible moment of indecision, of something like panic. She crowded it down and smiled at him. "Yes," she said.

The answer brought him embarrassment, for he wanted to kiss her and scarcely knew how to go about it. She lifted her head and made a slight motion with her hands, breaking his uncertainty, and he put his arms around her and gave her a soft kiss and stepped away. He was smiling and confused. "I've never done that before. I guess there's a lot of things I've never done." The deep-hidden New England humor began to sparkle in his eyes and the knowledge of his luck began to work slowly at him, building up his buoyancy. "Now, then, we've got to tell the Spicers."

"I don't know what Mrs. Spicer will say.

I promised to work a year for her."

"She's a good woman." Then he added in the considerate tone so characteristic of him: "If she won't release you from the promise, we'll have to wait, of course."

They found the Spicers in the kitchen; he was reading, and she knitting. Mrs. Spicer's glance searched them and her mouth settled with the thought that came to her. She laid her hands in her lap. "Spicer," she said, and when he lifted his attention from the paper, she nodded at the two younger people. Spicer looked around at them.

"Mr. Spicer," said Abbott Corning, "I'll be opening shop in the morning. I've not said this before, but I remember your kindness. Yours and Mrs. Spicer's. Now then . . ."

He looked at Katherine. "Is it the man or the woman who's supposed to say this?"

"It's plain on both of you," said Mrs. Spicer. "It needs no more saying."

"Well, now, that's good," said Spicer, and rose to extend his hand to both of them.

"Spicer," said Mrs. Spicer, "take Abbott out a moment."

She closed the kitchen door after the two men left. She wasn't pleased, Katherine thought. But it really wasn't displeasure so much as it was a fretfulness that gave her face an unhappier look. "Katherine, are you sure Ben won't come back? He might, mightn't he?"

"There's no use thinking about that."

"You still hope for it, don't you?" pressed Mrs. Spicer.

Katherine shook her head. "Maybe, in a little way, I do. But I know it's wrong. It's not practical. People have got to do the best they can, and not grieve over dreams. If they waited for their hopes to work out, nothing would get done and we'd all waste our lives. Maybe I'm a little bit sad, but I can get over it." She paused, still troubled by something in her mind. Then she said, "I have got to tell Abbott about Ben . . . before we're married."

"Why?" asked Mrs. Spicer, and watched Katherine with her insistent attention.

"It's important. He's got to know. That's fair."

"Katherine," said Mrs. Spicer, "I'm going to make you keep your promise. You've got to finish out your year with me."

"Why, then," said Katherine, "I shall. Abbott and I can wait."

She left the room, and presently Spicer came back and settled in his chair again to finish his newspaper. Mrs. Spicer stood at the kitchen window, staring through the pane to a night she couldn't see; and though

Spicer was an incurious man he finally became aware of her silence and looked up from his paper.

"Something not right?"

She was short with her answer. "Right or wrong, what's the difference?"

"You get thinking spells, Nelly. What do you think about?"

"Nothing," she said, and continued to look through the window.

Spring came with its warm rains and its sudden bright suns shining through an air washed clean. The pale greens of new growth made a lacework pattern against the dark greens of the land. The river lifted and turned yellow from the mud of caved-in banks; the pathways of the village sent up their thin steam as they grew dry. Abbott Corning built a shed at the back end of his store lot and bought a cow; early in the morning he milked it and drove it to a pasture out near the Terwilliger claim, and near suppertime he drove it back. He had left Mrs. Spicer's table.

"I could afford the board money," he told Katherine, "but I've got a debt to pay to the merchants in the East who trusted me. So it's better that I batch, though I do miss your cooking."

It became her habit then, on Sundays, to

go to his store and bake his bread and — knowing his liking for sweet things — a large cake with a butter frosting. On one such Sunday he hired a wagon and moved her packed things from the log cabin to the drier loft of his store.

"Maybe it will bring your family closer," he said. "You're the sort to remember your people. You got a long memory. I can see it in your eyes most any time."

She almost told him of Ben, but the impulse wavered and she postponed the ordeal. "It's a nice thing for you to take the space for my trunks," she said.

"Well, you don't ask much of anybody. I wish you'd ask more."

"I don't need much," she said.

He smiled at her. "You need whatever you'd want to ask for, and it would be my pleasure to supply it." He was embarrassed by the warmth of the statement. He looked down to the floor, softly adding, "Maybe I shouldn't trouble you with my feelings."

She touched his arm. "Abbott, I'll try hard to make things go well for us."

He said, "We've got six months to wait. I ought not grow impatient, but I do."

It was her turn to grow self-conscious, so much so that when they walked back to Spicer's she was glad to be in the shadows of the warm spring night. The bells of pastured cows rang gently and intermittently from the village edge and house lights seemed more than usually yellow in their shining. She stood a moment at Spicer's doorway, waiting for whatever he wished to say; but instead of speaking, he looked down to her with his quietness disturbed by the clear-shown impulse to kiss her. She said, "Good night," and turned quickly into the store.

She knew that was wrong and stood at her window to reason away the memories of Ben McLane which came without her permission. These would someday fade out, and then she'd smile at her foolishness, but it took so long a time. He was still important to her, and because he was important to her, she had to let him know. Sunday she'd do it.

She meant, on Sunday, to go to his store after breakfast work was done; instead he came to her.

"Day's fine," he said. "Northwest wind's blowing. Thought you might like to walk. The trails are dry up along the hill."

"Why," she said, "we'll take a lunch. I've never been up that hill." She rummaged a meal from the kitchen and packed it in a muslin sack and borrowed a pot for coffee.

They went by Spicer's store, where he stopped for a blanket, and then struck away from the town into the timber.

Though she had been in the village six months, she had never gone back to the little clearing in the timber where the emigrant wagons had camped; and when she came to it, she stopped and for a moment the picture came up full and strong of that wet morning, the wagons rolling away, and Mrs. Rowley crying, and Ben McLane disappearing into the shadows. She looked down at the round dark place where the fire had been. The taste of boiled wheat returned to her. Everything returned with its original sharpness.

"You're thinking again," said Abbott Corning. "It's like soot in your eyes."

"It's sad to think of people all scattered — the ones I knew so well."

"Well," said Abbott Corning, "it's a country for scattering. But it's a country for starting, and for coming together too. It's a good thing we're so busy out here that we've not got much time to think of the past."

"I've not had time yet to cry for my people," said Katherine.

"It was a bad thing," he said, his sympathy strong in his words.

They reached the mouth of a canyon

whose damp wild breath came downward to them; they found a trail along the hill's stiff slope, through masses of great fir trees. Wet rock faces glistened in the shadows and the fallen needles of a thousand years' accumulation made a carpet that gave with their weight. Near noon they came to a grassy summit at the peak of these hills and saw the land run away westward — black forest and green meadow and swelling domes of hills — until the massive wall of the Cascades rose up to top the eye. Directly below them the river flashed and turned its great loop, northward moving; beside the river was the small scar of Portland village.

They spread the blanket, made a fire to cook coffee, and had their lunch. Abbott Corning lay back with his sigh of fullest satisfaction, his eyes watching the fair sky. "I am a horse turned out for a day, and that's a good feeling."

"You work hard, Abbott. You keep long hours."

"I'm a slow man, and long hours don't hurt me. I'll never be great, Katherine, but I will be useful, and in time we ought to be well-fixed."

"You ought not speak of yourself so humbly."

"I couldn't fool myself," he said. "I do

admit that I have a business head. I do admit one other thing: I was a lonely man till I met you."

She knew this was the time to speak, but, looking at the contentment upon him, she could not bring herself to it. It struck her in the heart. She looked out upon the far mountains, telling herself that she would do it on the homeward walk.

"Abbott," she said, "you need more crockery in your stock at the store."

"It is not a day to think business," he said, and rose with a thought amusing him. "Now come look with me." She followed him to the break of the hill and sighted along his arm as he pointed toward the village. "See that little open spot beyond the Terwilligers', but short of the village? It is an acre, more or less, and five minutes' walk from the store. I have bought it. I should not have bought it without your seeing it, but the price was not much."

"It's your judgment," she said, and was warmed by his wanting to share the decision with her. "I see it. What's it for?"

"When the village gets larger," he said, "we'll not want to live in back of the store. We'll want a house which is not on the main street."

She said, "That will be a good thing. Is

there a sunny place for a garden?"

"You'll see," he said, and picked up the blanket and muslin sack. The secret amusement continued to bubble up and leave its impression on his face, and now and then he gave her a sly look. "It may please you," he said.

"I don't need to be pleased more than I am now."

"I wish you did," he said, and was wistful with his tone.

She said, very quickly, "I don't mean to be indifferent, Abbott. I'm not."

He went chuckling down the trail with her. They reached the canyon and walked toward town; when they were within a few minutes of it, Abbott Corning followed another trail into a grove of trees which soon began to thin out before a little meadow. "Now, then," he said, taking her hand, "will you close your eyes and let me bring you to it?"

He went before her and reached the clearing, and stopped in it. "If you like this," he said, "I'll be satisfied."

She opened her eyes to see the acre lying within the border of roundabout firs. A small creek crossed the clearing, wandering as it went; toward the middle of the acre stood three small cedars. This much she saw at first glance, and then her glance went beyond the cedars to a corner of the acre and discovered the plowed corner in which her father's seedling trees stood in their rows, one day to be an orchard.

He said, "I moved these at night, when you wouldn't notice. I hope I didn't do wrong. The house will sit by the cedars. You can look out of the window to the orchard, and there's your people with you, Katherine."

She turned to see the smiling gone from him completely. He was once more a sober man holding his hat in his hand, watching her with his hope for her happiness. She said, "Abbott," and began to cry. She tried to stop it by pressing her palms tightly against her eyes, but he reached up and pulled them aside and put his arms around her. He didn't say anything; he held her while she cried, his head touching the top of her head. All her restraint gave way before the pressure so long accumulated. She laid her arms on his shoulders to steady herself, and poured out everything bitter and regretful, and ceased to cry, and remained long still. He patted her slowly and lightly on the back; he waited, still without words.

She drew away and raised a reddened face to him, then realized how she looked, and turned aside to use her fingers to press away the tears. She kept her back to him, looking toward the nursery rows. "Well, Abbott, now I've cried for my people and I guess I'm done with it. I've been a sorrowful girl, but that's past."

He said, "I didn't do wrong, then?"

"No, Abbott. It was right."

He took her arm and walked back through the pathway and through the timber to the village. When they got to the door he stepped aside to let her go ahead of him. She stopped in the front room, but he went on to the rear with the blanket and left it and came back. He was restless and embarrassed, and he went by her and paused at the window, rattling the silver in his pocket. Suddenly he turned and stood in front of her with something of the expression she had noticed the night he had christened the building — the rash sparkling in his eyes, the boyishness, the close personal interest.

"Katherine," he said, "I'm not patient about waiting six months."

"Mrs. Spicer —"

He touched her arm, and hesitated, and pulled her forward. "No," he said, "it's a long time," and he kissed her with the driving impatience of a man in love.

It wasn't like his first kiss; it wasn't tender and embarrassed and unsure. He wanted her, and this possessiveness went around her like a heavy arm. She drew her head back, staring up to him; her lips softened from the knowledge of his wanting. She dropped her glance, smiling and unsteady.

"Well, then, Abbott," she said, "we must go see her."

"Now," he said. They crossed to Spicer's, and went through the front room, passing Spicer, who looked up with his incurious mildness. Mrs. Spicer was at the kitchen stove. She heard them, but some perversity made her delay turning around. When she did turn, with a wearied resentment on her face, she saw the pleasure in Katherine's eyes at once. She saw the change, and a loosening came immediately to those drawn cheeks; a kindness warmed her eyes.

"Mrs. Spicer —"

"You don't need to tell anybody," said Mrs. Spicer, "you've found a man."

"I found him a long time ago."

"No," said Mrs. Spicer, "you found him today." She looked at Katherine with her private message. She said, "Have you said what you thought you would say to him?"

"No," said Katherine. "It's not important. If it were important, I would. But it isn't at all."

Mrs. Spicer turned to the stove. She

opened the oven door and stooped to haul out a pan. "Well, then, I shan't keep you to a promise. You're sure it's all right?"

"Oh, yes," said Katherine, "it's all right. I'll be back in a little while to help with supper. I'll help as long as I can. I'll be close enough, even married."

"That's fine," said Mrs. Spicer, and went on with her work. She listened to the girl's steps and the man's steps go on to the store, and presently she straightened and stopped her work. There were tears in her eyes and she thought, *Sometimes it happens. Sometimes it's good like this.* She looked across the kitchen and out through the window, and for a little while she was quite still, with her thoughts far off and far back. She shook her head to clear her eyes, and turned to the stove.

Cry Deep, Cry Still

At four o'clock that morning when John Mercy rose to search out and yoke the oxen, it was a mud-black world. The scudding clouds of a southwest storm were breaking in violence against the hills and releasing a fat rain which searched through the cabin walls and became a humid sweat upon everything. Today would be only a sullen, end-of-the-world twilight, as yesterday had been, and for as many days back as Mrs. Mercy cared to remember.

Mercy returned for breakfast, the heat of the room dyeing his wind-stung cheeks to blood crimson. He said brief grace and looked about the table, to his wife Martha, to Caroline in her flannel nightgown, to young Tom still drugged with sleep. "The devil's crying at the eaves but he can't get in." The hard work of a first fall in Oregon, the laying up of the cabin and the breaking of land, had taken twenty pounds from him, but he was cheerful, his eyes as blue as old velvet. "I'll let Tom milk and fetch water. It will save me an hour. It's a slow sixty miles each way, the Yamhill and the Tualatin to

69

ford. They'll be high."

"You can't ford the Willamette or the Columbia," Mrs. Mercy said. "What'll you do?"

"At the Willamette's mouth I'll find some Indians to canoe me to the fort."

"And leave wagon and beasts for them to steal."

"I don't contemplate it," he said. "Eight days ought to see me back here."

"How can those pawky little canoes carry you, two mill-stones and a barrel of flour? You'll sink. What would we do, left three alone out here two thousand miles from home?"

"Don't contemplate that either," he said. He rose and made slow work buttoning on his overcoat while he watched his wife. "You'll be all right?"

"Worry for yourself."

"It might be nine days instead of eight," John Mercy said.

"If you see anybody along the way that we came over the plains with — though that would be like finding a penny in the ocean — tell them hello and say we're doing well."

"So we are," he said agreeably.

"Just say it," she retorted.

He went about the table to kiss the top of his daughter's head. He said, "Magpie for sharp," and he nodded at his son. "Do the chores without being asked and cause your mother no worry. You're the man here." He took up the sack of food and moved to the door, but there he swung to give his wife a grave moment's look.

She was aware of it and suddenly fell briskly to her chores about the fireplace, ignoring him. She said, "Well, you'd better get started," and then noticed the mud he'd brought into the house with his shoes. "Dirt, dirt, I'll die of it." He looked at her but said nothing, and went into the darkness.

Wind rushed past him with its fat, stinging rain. He threw the food into the wagon and walked abreast the oxen to prod them into motion. "Hup, Dandy, Babe! Hup!" The beasts stirred the covered wagon forward, into the meadow and across it toward a valley lying blind in the night.

Fort Vancouver, toward which he was bound for millstones and flour, was sixty miles northward through a country inhabited by scarcely more than a hundred white people; this was December and the year of 1842 came to its gusty ending in rain and wind. He bent his head and trudged forward over the spongy soil . . .

After he was well gone, Martha Mercy opened the door to look after him, sighting nothing now. She listened to the dashing roar of the wind in the fir tops high over the cabin; the sound of it drew her mouth into a displeased line and she closed the door and walked to the fireplace, a young woman with a clear brown face rarely lighted by a smile, with restless hands and a preoccupied manner. "Tom," she said, "the cow can hook off that top rail of the gate. You take a piece of rope and tie it."

The wind's rustling was endless, and she noted the glitter of water seeping through the log spaces. She turned to frown at the room: the beds and table and chairs cramping it, the boxes piled over boxes, the extra bedding and furniture stored above the rafter crosspieces, the crowded shelves, the clothing hanging from pegs everywhere; she saw the mud near the door and it was a match exploding her discontent, She seized the broom and went vigorously around the room, under the beds and under the children's feet at the table. Caroline said, "I want to dress now."

"Light the lantern, Tom. Put on the heavy coat."

She pulled the big kettle; with its simmering water, from the crane and scalded the milk bucket. Bundled against the weather, young Tom went out into the darkness and as soon as he had gone Caroline changed from nightgown to clothes.

Martha Mercy got the comb, and stood back of the chair for half an hour's patient combing of the girl's hair, forming its exact part, braiding it and tying the braids. Momentarily, she was pleased. Caroline was pretty.

"Now, then, if you're sharp as a magpie, as your father says, do the dishes," Martha said.

She went to the shed and carried in the full pans of another day's milk, took off the cream and dumped the skim into a bucket for the pigs; she scalded the pans and filled them with the fresh milk young Tom brought in. Young Tom went slowly out to feed the pigs, a first light then creeping like dirty water into the morning. She thought: *He's tired for some reason,* and began to worry about him; he never had Caroline's bubbling health.

She put on her big cloak and tied a scarf around her head. From the shed she got an armload of pitch wood and stove sticks and carried them to the outdoor fireplace. She laid the pitch wood, brought a bucket of coals from the cabin and got the fire going, the variable currents of wind throwing smoke into her face. When the fire was strong she hoisted a great iron scalding pot and lodged it on the rock ledge above the flame and took a bucket behind the cabin.

A barrel stood here on stilts, a tub beneath it. Fire ashes filled the barrel, the rain washed through the ashes, and lye water trickled into the tub; she made three trips from tub to kettle with the lye water, then got an egg from the house and dropped it in the lye water for a test. The egg floated, its end barely above surface. Out of the cabin she brought the grease saved from butchered deer, from two bears Mercy had shot, from bacon drippings. This went into the kettle with the lye water.

She fed the fire and stepped into the cabin, the lower half of her dress and her shoes sodden. The dishes were done, and Caroline stood dreaming at the fire.

"You take your book and go through your letters," said Mrs. Mercy.

"I'd rather make soap."

"You'll get to make it someday," said Mrs. Mercy, "and wish you didn't need to." She put on Mercy's extra pair of boots, her feet entirely lost within them, and returned to the kettle to find that the inslanting rain had dampened the fire. She brought more pitch kindling and chunks of dry fir bark from the shed. Tom watched her. She said, "Tom, take the milk clabber to the chickens. Count and see if they're all there — and get the eggs."

She fed the fire with wood standing ricked by the shelter, the sharp smoke making her cry. The morning moved on, such as it was. The plowed field beyond the foot of the hill — where winter wheat lay — was black as coal from its month long soaking; sullen clouds skimmed the earth and lodged in the timber so heavily that a fine fog sparked all about her. Young Tom returned from the chicken shed and ducked into the shelter of the cabin's doorway. "Six eggs, chickens all right." His face was solemn, his shoulders drawn up.

Trying to imitate his father, she thought, but she looked closely at him, not quite sure; this was the way he sometimes appeared just before coming down with a cold. She said, "Take the ax and go strip me some cedar bark, about this long." She spread her arms to indicate the length. "A lot of it."

"You'll kill the trees."

"We've got trees to kill," she said.

At noon the soap was half thick in the kettle, young Tom had stacked a pile of cedar bark in the back shed, and both of them were soaked. She made a meal of cold scraps and fried eggs and sassafras tea, immediately going back to the tedious chore at the fire. By four o'clock the soap was a clear, clean jelly the color of isinglass; she heard it splatter as it bubbled, and judged it right, and drew it from the fire, ladling the soap into the wooden tub. She stored the tub in the shed and returned to clean out the kettle while a premature night whirled down about the cabin.

"Time for milking, Tom."

After supper a greater wind and rain rushed against the cabin and stormed through the trees with the sound of a river cataract. She put Tom to his arithmetic and took the lantern out to look at the chickens huddled in their small house; still restless, she went to the corral to make sure Tom had tied the top rail well enough. To get anything in this country was very hard; to lose anything was a tragedy.

She went on to the store shed, playing the lantern's light along the shelves, over the salt crocks, the potatoes, cabbages and apples and pumpkins given them by their nearest neighbors, the Teals, four miles away. She brooded over the scantiness of the bacon and the half-empty salt-pork tub; it was six months before the garden came on or a hog could be killed, a close thing with four mouths to feed. When she stepped into the cabin she saw young Tom shiver and she knew that he was going to be sick.

"You go to bed."

She stood at the fire after both of them had settled for the night and gave Mercy a moment's thought, he camped somewhere in a dripping grove fifteen miles away; but he would be inside the wagon cover and he would be warm. She drew the fire together, laid her hand on young Tom's cheek, feeling no fever there yet, and snuffed out the lights. "Turn your back," she said to him and got ready for bed.

The firelight performed its golden, leaping dance on the walls. They were both young, but work was making them old too fast, all because Indiana had got too small for Mercy's notions and he wanted a mile of land in Oregon and his own grist mill. The endless rain was hard to bear, for it took her back to her home where the snow now was a shining crust on the ground and the cold wonderful air shook down the brown oak leaves, banking them in wind-rows against the rail-fence lines. She saw the little town with its houses spaced in their blocks, and the church bell's sound was strong in her ears. Past Pennoyer's, Gregg's and Jackson's she walked, rattling her knuckles against the fence pickets, over the packed snow to Burglon's store, whose shelves were so common then and seemed so rich now. Bob Burglon, learning the business from his father, waited on her; she stirred on the bed and closed him from her mind with effort.

Above the storm she heard a sound beginning, like the tearing of cloth. It grew suddenly to a snapping and whining, and she sat upright in terror and felt the cabin tremble — actually jump — as the tree struck close by with its roar and its dying shower of falling branches.

Caroline whimpered and young Tom woke and began to cough. She listened to her heart's pounding; wind yelled through blackness, and the blackness was heavier than lead. This was the hour when, no matter how she tried to stop it, she thought of Allen Mercy, born dead, lying inside the rail fence beyond the meadow. The blackness and the wet cold earth brought the thought to her.

Early on the fourth day she rose to make broth from a piece of salt meat simmered with potatoes and onions. On young Tom's waking she fed him against his will, but stopped when she saw he could hold no more down. Fever had cracked his lips, and his arms showed a first thinness, and though he was sleepy he could only catnap. She got Caroline's breakfast, took care of the milk and fed the chickens. Using two water buckets at a time, she made four trips to the creek, a hundred yards distant, to fill the water barrel in the shed; on her return from the final trip she found Caroline in the cabin's doorway, her eyes round as dollars.

"There's a dog. He went around back of the barn."

Mrs. Mercy dumped the water into the barrel. "There's no dog. There's nobody but the trapper yonder and he's got no dog. The Teals are across the river. It couldn't be their dog." Young Tom was at the moment sleeping and she hated to disturb him, but his face was so bright a red that she touched it with her hands. "There's no dog," she said.

"I saw him, right in the yard. He went back of the barn."

Mrs. Mercy looked at her daughter, shaken by a dreadful coldness. She pulled her into the cabin and closed the door and got the rifle from its pegs; she found a cap for the rifle's nipple. "Stay here till I come back and don't open the door." She let herself into the yard and stopped to look through the gray light, toward the meadow, toward the hills. She circled the house, half afraid to turn the corners, going on to the cowshed.

There was nothing to be seen between cabin and shed, and beyond the shed the trees cast a thick shadow. She swung to come straight upon the open door, to see inside the cowshed before she got too close to it; the cow stood forlornly there, disliking the rain. She drew a long breath of relief and walked toward the far side of the shed; before she got quite to its corner she caught sight of motion in the darkness of the trees, and a long, sunken-flanked wolf came silently into the clearing, saw her and stopped.

He was evilly thin, of a dirty, rusty gray, and his eyes were a strange green staring at her with an unhuman steadiness; he had a mind and he was thinking whether he should be afraid or whether he should jump at her — that she knew in the paralyzing moment of her stillness. She never thought of the gun in her hand, never realized she had it. She said, "You dirty thing — get!"

The sound of her voice startled the wolf. He made an easy turn of insolence and went shadowlike into the timber. Then she remembered she had a gun, but he was gone.

She ran to the shed, seized a piece of rope

and fixed it to the cow's halter, leading the cow to the cabin door and tying it there. When she opened the door, Caroline stood waiting.

"Where's the dog — why's the cow here?"

"If it was a dog, he might hurt the cow. I didn't see the dog."

She rested the gun beside the door. "Don't touch that." She went to the fire and rested her head against her hands to let the waves of weakness go through her. Maybe he wouldn't come this near to the house, but maybe he was hungry enough to dare; she had to leave the door open to watch the cow.

She turned, hearing Tom threshing on the bed. He was awake but he looked at her in a strange way and she knew the fever, still strong, made him lightheaded. It was more than a cold and he was in danger. She laid her hand softly on his chest, and he rolled his head, looking up to her with fear in his eyes.

"Am I going to die?"

"It's just a little thing. It's a cold. You've had colds before."

She held him up for a drink of water, pulled the quilt over him and briskly turned to her work. She made Caroline a bite to eat, she scalded the churn, and brought the milk from the shed; seated at the doorway, the churn between her legs and her eyes on the yard, she worked the dasher up and down.

Down the meadow, a voice hailed the cabin, shocking her, and in a moment Mrs. Teal, skirts dripping from a four-mile walk through wet meadow grasses, appeared at the door; with her was the oldest Teal boy, a basket in each arm.

Mrs. Teal said, "I missed your visit Sunday and got to wonderin'."

"Mercy's away to Fort Vancouver." A great relief from loneliness came upon Mrs. Mercy, so great that for an instant she was happy. But she could not reveal to this woman her weakness; she showed Mrs. Teal a steady face, and rose to accept the baskets with proper thanks.

"Just some garden things," said Mrs. Teal. "They'll rot in our storehouse, we've got so much. It'll be the same with you when your garden's started. First year's always a hard thing — nothing to do with." Mrs. Teal saw young Tom on the bed and walked over and bent and looked at him. Her voice was quiet: "What's ailin' him?"

"A cold," said Mrs. Mercy.

"If we just had some mustard for a plaster," said Mrs. Teal. "There's never anything. I'll be happy when there's a store."

She looked again at young Tom, silently and long; she was worried, Martha Mercy realized. The Teal boy stood beyond the doorway, waiting.

Mrs. Mercy looked at young Tom and Caroline and spoke to Mrs. Teal: "Maybe your son could take the gun and go look on the other side of the cowshed. There's a dog around." She added quietly: "A gray dog, Caroline thinks."

"Oh, dear," murmured Mrs. Teal. "They do bother in winter when they get hungry. Joe —" But Joe, reaching for the rifle, had already gone. "Have you got any turpentine? On a rag soaked with water, it would draw."

"No."

Mrs. Teal looked at her narrowly and lowered her voice: "You got another baby started?" When Martha Mercy shook her head, the other woman murmured, "Well, then it's weariness. You been up most of the night, I guess. That's a terrible big tree that fell. Mercy better clear more away. I'll leave Joe here to sleep in the shed tonight. And to fetch me if you have need."

"It's a trouble for him."

"Great stars!" said Mrs. Teal. "What's people for? And there's no need to stand off. Not out here. People have got to have each other. Even if they don't like each other, they

83

got to get along. Well, it's soon dark and I'll go." She gave a last look to young Tom and went into the yard, calling to her son. Joe Teal appeared from the timber a moment, listened to his mother's words, and went back into the timber, as lean and easy and insolent as the wolf itself.

Martha Mercy sat down before the churn, lifting and lowering the dasher in steady rhythm. Covertly from time to time Mrs. Mercy threw a glance toward young Tom. The fever was growing, the breaking point hadn't been reached. She kneaded the butter and took it to the storehouse, poured buttermilk into a jug and brought young Tom a glass of it; when she lifted him upright to drink she felt the fiery heat of his body. He drank the full glass and fell back on the bed, fretful and weak. She brought up the quilts around him.

Darkness came down with a rising wind and rain. She made supper for Caroline and for Joe Teal, who, coming out of the darkness, ate as though in a haste to be back at his hunting. "I'll sleep in the cowshed," he said, and took a blanket from her and led the cow away. She ate nothing, having no appetite. She washed the dishes, combed and put up Caroline's hair and sent her to bed.

"The light's in my eyes," said Tom.

She snuffed the candles and drew a chair beside young Tom's bed, holding his hot hand. "Now, then," she said, "you'll be better in the morning. This fever's about burned out the corruption, and then it'll go and you'll eat like a pig." His breathing was fast and heavy, the labor of it exhausting him; his heart alarmed her with the violence of its pulsing against his skin.

A terrible helplessness came upon her and out of it came bitter thoughts and a moment of hatred for John Mercy. He was an ambitious man who couldn't abide the thought of being small in Indiana — believing that a mile of land, a mill and someday a store out here would make them happy and leave the children well off. But what good was that to young Tom now, half dead with fever? It wasn't a healthy country, no freezing weather to kill the putrid things in the earth and air each year, only this wetness which sickened people and kept them damp winter long.

In sleep, young Tom cried. She sat in the slowly chilling room, listening to the fever have its way, holding his hand and silently praying her will into him. She feared to let his hand go and she feared to move. Mercy,

85

about now, would be starting back over a country without roads or bridges; she had no tenderness in her thinking of him, only a feeling that if young Tom should die, her mind would die.

Pain struck her in the back of the neck, and she seized the edges of the chair to avoid falling. She had slept a few moments and her hand had fallen away from young Tom's hand. She searched for it, and panic came upon her at the quietness that was upon him. She bent, placing her head near his face; his breath rustled against it, but the sound of hard struggle was gone; and when she touched his face the heat, too, had gone.

He was motionless; he was in the sleep of exhaustion and the fever was broken. She pulled the covers around him and, removing only her shoes, she got into bed beside Caroline and lay awake, too tired to be relieved . . .

On the seventh day the rain stopped; and the water-beaded trees around the house were all asparkle. A wolf hide hung in the cowshed, shot by Joe Teal, who had gone home. Young Tom sat propped around with pillows, his eye sockets deep and a waxiness on his face, too weary to complain at being in bed; but he was hungry and he was better.

She carried ten pails of freshet-yellowed

water from the Cobway and set on the wash-tub. "You're not so sick you can't do some studying," she told him. "It's time wasted that's sinful, and I'll not have you ignorant like that trapper. Caroline, get that arithmetic book for him." She hoisted the boiling tub to a bench before the door, and, her skirts tied up, she did the washing.

Joe Teal slipped into the cabin with a bottle of berry wine sent by his mother, having covered the four miles like a hound and yet breathing softly; and he refused food and quietly disappeared.

By afternoon the washing hung from every overhead pole in the cabin, beneath which she had to duck to make a meal and tend young Tom. The closeness of this living crossed her and made her more and more irritable. This was her mood when a straight, thin and whiskered man in a dark suit so old and hard-used that it had a green cast to it stepped from a horse before her door and cheerfully announced himself.

"I am Reverend White, ridin' my circuit," he said. "Sister Teal said you were here. Boy's better? This, I guess, is Caroline, and I've struck you at washin' time and you won't like me for it."

She didn't. It offended her enormously to bring him into this room with its crowded furniture, and its damp clothes scraping the top of his gray head. But he was a minister and she was courteous to him, by nature respecting his profession. She went hastily around to make up a meal which, because of its poor showing, further depressed her. He ate and he talked and he was full of good spirit.

"Husband be back soon? It's a long ride to Vancouver. Sister Teal mentioned he was after millstones. A miller by trade?"

"He's got knowledge of it," said Mrs. Mercy.

"He'll make out, he'll do well. He's got good land, good water power — he's had the best choice before the multitude come. There's no land like it for richness." He gave her a passing glance and went back to his food. "A little rain, of course. There's the gift it's got — water to make things grow. I recall the harshness of Northern winters."

"I pine for cold weather," she said.

"That's natural, but another year here and you'll not hanker for home and friends. You'll have them here."

"Will they ever come?"

"By the thousands," said Reverend White, "and if you bend your ear, sister, you can hear the tramplin' of their feet now. It's destiny. That winter wheat planted in the field?"

"Yes."

"The rain that troubles you will bring that wheat on fat and heavy. The rain is your bread and butter." He looked at the wine bottle on the table; she felt shame that he should see it and wondered what his thoughts were.

"That's Sister Teal's elderberry, I recognize. No medicine like it for your son."

"Could I offer you some, Reverend?"

He said, "No," in a rather reluctant way and at once said it stronger. "No. Barely enough for him. Now then," he said rising, "it's twenty miles to the next family and I have got to ride." He laid a hand on young Tom's head, on Caroline's head, his hands blackened from the reins of the horse.

He was a minister, but he had none of that refinement about him which, in Indiana, sets ministers apart; he was a man before a minister, more like a millwright than anything else. He thanked her for the meal and rode downgrade to the meadow and out of sight. She was disappointed because he had neither asked anything of her spiritual condition nor had knelt with them in prayer.

She would have been surprised at the Reverend White. Passing around a point of the hill he came to a grove of oaks well beyond the cabin, here dismounting to kneel before a tree. He knew her story from Mrs. Teal, he knew her trials from the trials of other women before her and he knew, by her expression, the depth of her unhappiness. Knowing it, he prayed for her aloud, naming all the troubles she had undergone and all the excellences he saw within her. He listed them in a good round voice to God, stating her case as a lawyer might have done; and in the same voice he asked for a small amount of forgiveness, for a great deal of help. Then he rose, brushed his wet knees and rode into the gathering twilight toward a cabin twenty miles away . . .

She milked, fed the pigs, and gathered the eggs and locked in the chickens after counting them. After Caroline had gone to bed she got her basket and pulled the rocker to the fire — all the long day waiting for this restful moment — and settled there with thread and patch cloth. For a moment the redness of her hands drew her attention and she let them lie while she became aware of the scratches upon them. She remembered that her grandmother's hands had been like this, but not her mother's; for her grandmother had gone through the same drudgery while her mother, marrying the village merchant, had lived a calm life.

She might have married a merchant, too, and her days would have been as pleasant as her mother's. All day long the voices of the town would be around her, leaving no room for lonesomeness, and she would belong, she would dance, she would go to church. She had not let herself think too much of Bob Burglon — that was a kind of unfaithfulness; but now she let him come into her mind; his courtship sent its sweetness through her as she recalled it.

It was hard to know, sometimes, what put one man above another and why John Mercy, so abruptly coming into her life, had made Bob Burglon seem no longer right. It had been clear enough then. She looked closely at Bob Burglon, she looked closely at her husband — and she said silently, "No more of that," and put it out of her head. The fireplace light at last made her eyes tired and she went to bed . . .

She was up still earlier next morning and by daybreak had finished the never-changing chores. Now she brought in from the shed the slabs of cedar bark young Tom had cut, and began pounding the cedar fiber free, at last having a pile of it and a great mound of fluff around her. She brought out a loom, tacking on the stringy cedar twine as warp, and began the tedious hand job of running the woof through; by noon she was sorry she had begun and grew cross when young Tom became hungry. "Caroline, fix his big stomach something."

She hated to waste time, and by two o'clock, having had no meal herself, finished the cedar mat, threw it on the floor before the doorway and was done with it. But for a moment she studied it and thought: *Why, it's not bad,* and saw how she could do better next time. She was in haste; everything piled up on her. From the shed she got a venison joint, and put it into the deep skillet. She made a pie, and at proper time laid onions and potatoes and parsnips around the baking venison. Twilight came on, she turning rapidly from one piece of work to another.

She changed young Tom's bed, washed his face; she did Caroline's hair and was momentarily happy with her daughter's prettiness; and then at last she did her own hair and tied on a new apron. It was full dark by that time; standing at the open doorway she listened for the sound of Mercy's wagon to rise from the far deep quiet of the night. She began to worry, to see the rivers he had to cross, the Indians who went back and forth through this country in their roving bands. Young Tom said, "It's way past suppertime."

"You can wait a little longer," she said: then, in the distance beyond the meadow, she heard Mercy's call. "It will be just a little while," she said. She looked at them, adding, "We will not say we've been troubled, mind you." She looked from one to the other. "I want you to know that there's always trouble, and each one has got to stand his own, or everybody'd always be crying. Your father's got his, and bears them, and we'll bear ours."

He circled the wagon into its place beside the cabin, seeing his wife and daughter framed in the doorway's gushing yellow light. He said, "That's a pretty sight. Everything well?"

Mrs. Mercy said, "We got along."

"I said eight days — and eight days it was."

"You can thank the Lord as much as your own guessing," she said. He unyoked and led away the oxen and came slowly back, walking with a weary man's loose knees. He got something from the wagon and said to Caroline, still standing in the doorway, "Magpie," and saw young Tom in bed. "What's here?"

"He had a cold," said Mrs. Mercy, "but it's all right now. We'll eat when you've washed." She looked at him, knowing he had spared no strength to be back on time; he met her glance and a sparkle got into his eyes and he said, "Well, then, I've not been missed?"

"Don't be foolish, Mercy. It's not right to beg for sentiment." She watched him reach into the package he carried, laying out a clustered chunk of transparent rock candy, and a string of Hudson Bay beads. "Candy, from London, for the kids. Beads for you. Pretty things."

She looked at them, she didn't touch them, she didn't meet Mercy's eyes. Her manner was brisk, almost impatient. "I hope you didn't waste money on me. You know I don't year trinkets. They will do for Caroline," she added and turned to bring the roast to the table.

He sat heavily on the rocker and got out of his boots, into his slippers. He washed and combed his hair and took his place at the table. When his family had come about it, he looked at them, one by one, and dropped his head.

"For the food, for a safe return, and for the health of this family, Lord, thanks, Amen." He raised his head, a steady faintly austere benevolence coming to his face. "No trouble, then?"

"Nothing to speak of," said Martha Mercy.

Quarter Section on Dullknife Creek

They dropped from the high hills to the top of a lower ridge, Tom Baker and his son Elzie, and left the horses and stopped by a big pine. Elzie leaned against the pine, holding the Krag. For a boy of twelve it was a bulky gun but the weight didn't seem to bother him; nothing bothered him now because he was all tied up in the hope of getting his first deer. The sun was almost down and the light had changed, filling the ravine below them with dusty pearl-gray shadows; down there was a runway that mule deer used in coming and going from the hills.

"In fact," said Tom Baker in a voice very soft for so big a man, "there's a buck movin' out of the brush now. You see him, Elzie?"

Elzie lifted the Krag along the pine bark and steadied it. His heels squirmed slowly in the dust; he was bracing himself against the Krag's recoil, for he had practised on this gun long enough to know the wallop it had. "But I believe I'd wait," said Tom Baker in the same gentle murmuring, "till he got lower in the canyon. He ain't seen us and he can't smell us and he'll drift down and come to a stop, to look things over. That's the way they travel. Stop and look and go — and stop again. Same way when they reach water — a drink and a look, and a drink and a look. Aim right behind the forequarter. Don't want to gutshoot him."

He watched Elzie, not the buck. Elzie's cheek lay flat against the gunstock and his whole face was solemnly thin, which would be a youngster's excitement freezing everything inside him. A man had to remember the way a boy felt when he was twelve, shooting his first deer or doing anything for the first time. A man needed to remember about being young, because it was so easy to forget. Elzie's sighting eye ceased to wink and the crook of his finger grew steadily smaller against the trigger. The report of the gun was a dry burst which fled through the hills in loosening waves and died out as fragments in far corridors. The buck jumped and dropped, not moving again. Elzie worked the Krag's bolt but he held the gun half lowered, staring at the brown patch of the deer below; his face was starved and thoughtful, his eyes black as coal.

"Wait up," said Tom Baker, so gently, and walked to his horses for a rope. It was a mighty big feeling for a youngster, that first kill; it just went right down to the roots. You wouldn't ever think it from looking at Elzie's small and pointed face just now, but that was being young, to hold the big feelings out of sight. The little feelings always showed but not the big ones. He came back with the rope and they went down the slope together, Elzie circling the buck.

"Not at the head, son. Don't get in front of those horns till we know." When he tested the deer with his boot he knew it was stone dead; and cut its throat at once. He waited to see if Elzie remembered how he had been taught and when the boy turned over the safety on the Krag and laid it down, he was pleased. Training took a lot of time, but when you saw the results work out, you got a kind of grateful feeling. He said: "A mighty square shot. You did well. And there's our winter's venison as good as in the jar right now."

Praise always affected Elzie. He looked down and said in a half-smothered way: "Did just like you said. Didn't waste a shot, did I?"

"No sir, you sure didn't," said Tom Baker. He opened the deer, cleaning it. He broke a branch from the nearest pine and trimmed out a couple of short poles, cutting them to a point at each end and jamming them in the buck's tendons. He threw one end of the rope over a taller limb of the pine, fastened the other end to one of the poles, and hauled the buck well off the ground, tying the free end of the rope to another pine. "High enough to keep the coyotes off. It will cool tonight. Some men," he added, "hang their meat other end down. I like this way best; seems as though it drains better."

He explained these things in a deliberate, patient way, so that they would sink in. For he had a humble man's deep respect for the usefulness and the power of knowledge. He had no book learning he could give his son; all he knew were the practical things, the lessons he had learned by the usage of his hands, and these he meant Elzie to have; because they were all he could give, and because the giving of them might save Elzie some of his own toil.

The sun dropped and twilight moved in swiftly, a bodiless gray water filling the canyon brimful. Tom Baker wasted another few moments to roll a smoke, so that Elzie might have the last spell of pleasure from looking at his deer. Then they climbed the canyon's side, got to their horses and descended the long grade toward the floor of the sage desert.

Now that it was over, Elzie thawed and became talkative. He said: "It was a good one, wasn't it? What'll it weigh?"

"Dress close to two-fifty."

"You got sharp eyes, dad. I wouldn't of seen it until you spoke. Then I just remembered what to do. I just remembered what you'd said. Seems like I had to remember everything at once, and then I did. About the trigger and keeping my eyes open and takin' time, and sighting behind the forequarter. I used to wonder how I'd be able to see that spot. Now I know how it goes. Next year I'll know how to dress it, too."

"Sure," said Baker. "It's the knowin' that counts, Elzie. You read a thing and then you see it. But you've got to do it. Then you really know."

The sage desert opened below and beyond them, with twilight's dark-opal haze shimmering on it, with here and there a faint light glittering from wide-spaced homestead houses, and the black hulk of the Rim rising as a solid shadow thirty miles west. Dropping from the bench of the hills, they forded Dullknife Creek, crossed the road and came to the yard and the house. Lissie and Little Bill were making a clatter inside but Mrs. Baker was in the doorway, saying: "Any luck?"

Baker saw the struggle on Elzie's face —
to shout it out at once or to hold himself in.
Elzie held himself in, saying in as deep and
brief a voice as he could manage, "We got
one."

"Elzie's deer," softly added Tom Baker.
"Nice one."

"Now, Elzie," applauded Mrs. Baker's
voice, but Elzie was gone, kicking his horse
toward the corral. Tom Baker grinned at his
wife, and put away the horses. Elzie drove
in the cow and mixed up the mash for the
hogs while Baker milked, his big hands
squeezing the jets in tinny rhythm against
the sides of the pail. He strained the milk in
the pantry shed and poured it into the shallow skim pans, whereupon would come by
morning the thick rise of yellow cream; and
washed at the back porch basin, blowing the
water through his hands as he scrubbed his
face. Elzie was inside speaking to seven-year-
old Lissie and to Little Bill who couldn't
catch on, being only two: "Well, it came
down the canyon and dad saw it and I shot
it. Just one shot." He put out his hand,
cocking thumb and forefinger and said:
"Bang."

Little Bill said: "Bang."

"Ah," said Elzie, "you're just a kid."

Tom Baker chuckled behind his towel. He

went into the yellow light of the kitchen, into its warm smell of supper; and sat up to the table. He said, "Your turn, Elzie," and bowed his head a little, winking at Lissie while Elzie said grace.

Mrs. Baker said: "Tomorrow will be a good day to work on that meat. Bring it down early, Tom."

When they had finished, Tom Baker brought in a boiler of water and set it on the stove; and dragged the galvanized washtub to the center of the floor. He settled long-legged in a chair and lighted up a pipe, a man cast upon the shores of indolent content. He had a little plowing to do, a load of wood to bring out of the hills, and a few beeves to sell; but then the work of the year was about done and he could look either backward or forward and feel no worry. There was food and shelter, and no debts, and everybody was in good health. Mighty strange how these plain things counted to a man. These above everything else. The smoke of his pipe drifted over the room in sleazy layers and a haze of steam began to rise from the boiler. Little Bill crawled into his lap, reaching for his pipe stem. Lissie stood on a chair to wipe dishes, and Elzie was outside in the glow of moonlight; he would be dreaming over the day, living every minute of it again, just growing big with it. You had to remember how youngsters felt.

He put Little Bill in the chair, dumped part of the hot water into the tub, and re-filled the boiler; he rolled back his sleeves, and undressed Little Bill and knelt down, the pipe angled at a corner of his mouth. Little Bill was round-bellied, full of the devil and as slippery as the bar of soap; when he had finished his chore, buttoning on Little Bill's nightgown, Tom Baker was wet to the armpits. Afterwards, dumping the tub and adding fresh water, he gave Lissie her bath; and called Elzie in.

Elzie took his own bath, making work out of it. He was pretty close to twelve, flat-sided and skinny-muscled as boys get to be at that age, the skin on his stomach white in con-trast to the turned tan of his arms and legs and neck. Lissie sat, half sleepy, in Baker's lap and Little Bill, holding the edges of his nightshirt from the damp floor, slowly cir-cled Elzie in the tub; he pointed his finger at Elzie and said: "Bang — bang."

Elzie said: "You ought to send these kids to bed. I'm gettin' pretty old to be stared at."

Baker's glance lifted over Elzie's head, to his wife watching in the background. "For a fact, I guess you are."

It took time to get all this done and some-times it dragged when you were tired. But, herding the youngsters up the stairs, with Little Bill riding his back, he figured it was something you had to stop and think about. They wouldn't be young long; soon enough they'd be out of his reach for good. So the time to make them remember, to see they learned the right things and saw the proper examples, was now — in this short space you had with them. He listened to their prayers and opened the attic windows and left the lamp low-burning on account of Little Bill, its faint light making all the shad-ows of the attic darkly mysterious. He kissed Little Bill and Lissie, smelling the soap on them and the rank, sweet odors below the soap fragrance, which was the smell of child-hood; and scrubbed Elzie's black hair with his hand. He hadn't kissed Elzie for a couple of years now, knowing the boy was a little old for it. "Well, maybe if we need a little fresh meat we'll go after another one late this month." He walked downstairs, dumped the tub and refilled the boiler, and went out to sit on the porch, nursing his pipe. In a little while his wife joined him.

The hard heat of the year was gone; this was Indian summer, with haze closing over the land and the smell of smoke abroad and the kind of a quietness that comes when the earth slows down and steadies itself for winter. He felt an edge in the small wind — the edge of coming rain. Crickets were singing and the frogs had begun to make their pleasant sawed-off racket down in the quiet willows where Dullknife Creek made its slackwater pool. The moon was a quarter full and this light silvered the thick dust of the Prairie City road and lay on the rising benchlands like a depthless mist. In this night the land gave up its thick scents, or sage and stubble field and stacked hay and barnyard and dust and wild rose and the sweet Williams growing by the gate. He had lived with them so long he could catch each smell distinct and clear from the others. A night like this took all the trouble out of a man's bones; the last murmuring of the children was pleasant to hear in the stillness.

He laid the flat of his heavy hand on his wife's knee, turning slowly to see her. There wasn't anything easy about a woman's life on a sagebrush quarter section; but she still stayed young, she still had her quick humor — and a sort of swing and sparkle to her. Her hair was very black and after twelve years of marriage she held her strong, soft-rounded shape, so that even now it stirred him when he thought about it, as it had before marriage. He liked her steadiness, he liked her fun; he liked the way she still could flirt with him, holding him off and then, when it got exasperating, coming to him and making everything all right. It never got calm and settled, never dull; there was still that hunger underneath.

He tapped his pipe on the toe of his boot and went in to pour his bath water, and to refill the boiler for her. The tub was always a problem for a man his size. He sat jack-knifed in it, his toes jammed against the sides, his back creased into the rim, feeling pretty awkward and wryly grinning back at her open laughter at the sight he made; she knelt and scrubbed his back and dripped water perversely on his face and left him. When he was through he emptied the tub and refilled it for her; and went around the house, trying the windows and doors, and took the clock and wound it, and went to bed.

Lying there, thinking back over the year, he saw nothing to be disturbed by. For a man who had come off the open range, salty and a little wild twelve years before, he had done well. When she came to bed, warm and close and her hair damp and sweet-smelling, he said:

"Next week we'll just load up the wagon

and go up into the hills for a vacation."

Her laughter, quick and like a summons, turned him. "For an old woman," he said, "you're pretty fresh."

"Next week's next week."

"Sure," he said, "and this is now."

He went into the hills at first daylight and brought out the buck; and strung it up in the woodshed and skinned it, with Elzie watching. Baker said: "Keep a heavy pull on the hide. Stretches the tallow from the skin and gives you a clean cut." He halved the carcass and butchered it on the chopping block, taking off the quarters, slicing the steak meat, and trimming the ribs. His wife already had jars boiling and the frying pan on the stove. The steaks would be fried, they'd go in gallon jars, sealed in their own gravy; the chuck meat she'd make into meat balls, using the tallow to cover them; and she had a way of putting part of it up in brine, so that nothing was wasted. The last thing he did was to cut long strips of flank meat to be put in the smokehouse and jerked. He got the smokehouse fire started, left Elzie in charge and, with a remaining quarter wrapped in a clean muslin sack, he lined out for town.

He left the quarter at Mrs. Tyson's, four

miles down the road, and reached Prairie a little beyond noon. He saw Pete Luz about selling his four cows, bought a few things his wife had asked him to get and got a bag of candy apiece for the children. Roundup time was a week away and somebody had put a couple of banners across the street, giving this raw, wooden town an overdressed air. There was a Sunday crowd in the saloon, homesteaders and riders from the cattle out-fits. He knew most of them, saluted them cheerfully and had a drink or two, passing the time of the day and catching up on the gossip. In the middle of the afternoon he thought about eating and started over to the Shorthorn. Somebody said, "Hello, Tom," and he stopped to talk to Ned Puryear and then saw the banker's boy, Jimmy Ryan, come riding down the street on a good horse and a new saddle.

Jimmy Ryan was around twelve, same as Elzie, and he was a smart young fellow, tak-ing some pleasure in showing off the horse and the saddle. Puryear said: "Where'd you get the saddle, Jimmy?"

"Birthday," said Jimmy and held a tight bit on the horse, making it fiddle-foot in the dust.

The saddle, Tom Baker saw, was straight out of the shop, and expensive, with acorns stamped in and round skirts and decorated stirrup leathers and fenders. Jimmy Ryan went down the street, the horse dancing sidewise in the dust, and on that instant a feeling, quick and cold and disheartening, shook its way through Tom Baker. He forgot about the Shorthorn, about being hungry. He stood there, staring at the boy until the boy was gone; and swung on his heels to get his packages from the saloon, returning to his horse. This was the way he looked in the saddle, a heavy-thewed, limber man with his skin smooth and sunbrown, and a long pair of lips settled across heavy teeth, and a loose-brimmed hat raked over his hair, which was black as dye. He sat there, staring at the candy he had bought and change went through him completely. The liquor had loosened him, but when he came to think of Jimmy Ryan, and the saddle, and the three bags of candy in his hand, he wasn't loose any more. He rode slowly home.

The youngsters were happy about the candy but that didn't help him. His wife had a side-table full of canned venison and he said in the soft voice which never left him, "That's sure nice," but emptiness rattled inside Tom Baker and his wife saw it and took time to come to the door and watch him when he crossed the yard. He relieved Elzie at the smokehouse, building up the fire; he stood at the fence and looked across the quarter section; he rolled a cigarette and just stood there, with the points of his shoulders dropped, as though the heart had gone out of him.

The sun went down and supper time came. He sat at the table, a changed man who said nothing while he looked at Elzie and the younger ones; and afterwards he built a smoke in his pipe and went to the porch. He didn't lean back in ease. He humped forward, his long arms rested on his legs, hands down, staring out at the land through the tobacco smoke. It was funny what a day did to a man. Now this had looked pretty nice last night, this quarter section by moonlight. It didn't look that way now. It wasn't exactly the saddle; Elzie had a good enough saddle even though it was old and plain. Well, it was what the saddle meant. Ryan had something to give his son, Ryan would send the boy away to school and Jimmy would keep up with things, the way Ryan had. It was a matter of learning; you weren't anything in the world without learning; not the way the world went now.

He listened to the children as they climbed the stairs, not following them as he usually did. His wife finished the dishes and came out to sit beside him, waiting through his silence; she was, he realized gratefully, an understanding woman. She knew he was in trouble and waited until he spoke it.

When a man felt satisfied he never saw much; it took trouble to open his eyes. Right now he was remembering his boyhood and the two-room log house in Montana which had somehow held his parents and five children, and a grandfather, who slept in the barn. They had a small outfit and they got along; but when they grew up it was his oldest brother Pete who took the ranch. It wasn't big enough to support anybody else and so the rest of the young ones just drifted away; some of them he had never heard from since, nor had he ever written back. That's the way it was.

And that's the way it would be here. This quarter section on Dullknife Creek wasn't much to pass on; looking through the moonglow, he saw it pretty straight — just a sagebrush outfit, with his kids growing up to nothing, and drifting, and not knowing enough to be anything better than he had been or his father had been. And never writing back.

He sat there, miserably seeing it; and spoke. "Well, it was just a saddle Ryan gave his boy, Jimmy. Never mind the saddle. It's

111

Ryan standing behind Jimmy, able to give him something and send him out to school. You could see that on Jimmy when he was sittin' in the saddle — a sort of top man look. He knows he's on the right track, goin' somewhere. It shows up. What've I got to give Elzie, or Little Bill? What's ahead for Lissie? No, I got to find a way. I got to get some money. No use sittin' around here all winter." And presently he added in the slow way of a man who had made up his mind: "In the mornin' I'll pack a blanket roll and go over to that railroad construction outfit. Man can always get on there."

He was gone by daylight, hiking the thirty miles, and was on the construction company's payroll that same afternoon, handling a shovel at three dollars a day. They were cutting a grade down the face of the Rim — one long slash to let the new railroad off the high desert to the Prairie City level. He paid six bits a day for board and bunked in a shanty that had a tin stove and double decked bunks and a card table and a couple chairs; you could smell the staleness of tobacco and whisky and unwashed clothes and blankets. In this particular shanty were three Irishmen, a Lithuanian, a Mexican and a dangerous kid that called himself Calumet Red.

Three hundred men worked on the grade; they were coming and going all the time. On the second day the strawboss came by. "You're a rancher — you handle horses?"

"Sure."

"All right, you drive team. You're on the hook at five and a half a day."

The teamsters worked up and down the raw powder-gray dust of the grade, hauling water and supplies. The work wasn't any harder but it brought in two-and-a-half more a day. That was what knowledge did for a man. If you knew how to do something, you got out of the crowd; you climbed up. He could handle horses. It wasn't so much — but it just showed what knowledge did. He'd have to tell Elzie about this, so Elzie would understand what it meant to know something. Now and then, driving the grade, he watched the superintendent, Mr. Cochran, hurry along the cut; a solid little man, quick as a terrier, with his eyes moving around, sharp and observant. That's the thing he must tell Elzie. Even a humble man with a little knowledge got his rewards; but then you learned more, like Mr. Cochran, and you rose up over three hundred men, or a thousand, or more.

It just depended on how much you knew.

But it was hard to stick out that first week. He missed his wife and he missed the children; and he worried a little at not being around to talk to Elzie — just to slip in a word now and then, so that Elzie might catch something he wouldn't otherwise get. About growing up, about what was the right thing and the seemly thing, about what was straight and what was not. This mighty short time in childhood was all you had to set them out with their feet in the right direction. It was hard to be here and feel this time slip away. He sat in a bunkhouse chair by night, or lay on his bunk and smoked his pipe, all his muscles heavy with weariness, listening to the men in the shanty; and watching Calumet Red. The kid had a swagger and he was insolent. Blond hair grew down like a woolly mat in the back of his neck and he had thick shoulder muscles and there was a stain of red in the corner of his eyeballs, and he had the men bluffed, even the Lithuanian who was a giant. Calumet Red was maybe twenty and once or twice Tom Baker saw the kid turn his pale, red-shot eyes on him; as though sizing him up to see if he could bluff him, or lick him.

Saturday noon at the end of work he lined out for home, walking fast. It was dark when he came down the last turn of the road and the light from the house made him feel odd; he had never been away from his family this long before and now that light seemed to shine against him, as though he were outside of it. It came quickly, and quickly went away. The door was open and his wife stood in it, waiting and smiling, with her head tipped aside. When he came to her he felt awkward, like a stranger, and he stood there and at last said: "Well, don't look like anything burned down." But she laughed at him, or with him, and put her hand on his shoulder and kissed him.

"I've saved up some supper. I knew you'd be here."

The kids were in bed. Baker got a towel and a bar of soap and went down to the creek and took his bath in the pool. The day had been warm and the water was warm, and he went back to the house and ate his supper, with his wife seated opposite, chin in her hands, watching.

"Elzie's done all the milking."

"He'll do," said Baker. It was good to be here; it was a feeling in his bones, like rest. He built a smoke in the pipe and wiped dishes while she washed, and walked around the yard in the moonlight, looking at the horses in the corral, scratching the back of the sow in the pen. The smell of sage came off the desert rank and satisfying and the benchland rolled upward in the silver yellow glow toward the pines. He returned to the house and went up to the children; he opened the attic window wider and looked down at them, at Little Bill who lay on his back with his arms flung out and every muscle loose, at Lissie's yellow hair tumbled around her head, at Elzie whose face showed a patch of dirt on one side of his freckled cheek. They were asleep, they were dreaming. In bed, he lay awake beside the warmth and the softness of his wife, with her head lying on his shoulder, and silence came down wonderfully — the silence of a house filled with a family all together.

In the morning he worked at the little chores and chopped wood. There was still the smell of rain in the air. "One good soakin' and I'll take a day off to plow," he said. They had chicken and gravy and mashed potatoes and biscuits and pumpkin pie for noon meal; and then it was time to go. But he loitered around the house, just walking in and out of it until it was three o'clock. "Well," he said, "I'll be back next week," and left his wife at the door. The youngsters walked down the road with him a mile or more, and then he went on alone.

At the big dip in the road he turned to see them standing far behind. They were three in a tapering row, all holding hands, Elzie and Lissie and Little Bill; he raised his hand at them and set out to cover the distance. It was a long thirty miles.

First fall rain set in that week, coming up out of the south west in long slantwise ropes glittering like ragged splinters of glass against the leaden day. The powdery gray alkali mud deepened on the grade and water stood in the ruts until the wagon hubs touched it; and this mud and this wetness was on everything. That following Saturday it was too stormy to go home; and he sat through Sunday in the bunkhouse, idle and irritable, smelling the damp steam rising out of clothes and the smell of unwashed bodies and listening to the broken stories of the men around him. He sat there, far away from all of them, while he thought of his family, and a jumpiness got into him. Calumet Red, coming to the stove, pushed him accidentally, perhaps, back in the chair, and stared at him with his red-stained eyes. "Why in hell you got to take up all this space?" And the kid seemed to wait, with his lips puckered back from his bad teeth.

Baker let that pass, though he knew he should have called the kid at once; there was always that slow way of judging in him. Then it was Thursday with all the world drowned out in gray rain mists and the bunkhouse was like a steam bath, close and rank and dismal, and everybody was on edge. There was a bunch of Russians in the next shanty, all good men, but they had gotten some whisky and now were singing in a wild low way that clawed at the man's nerves. Tom Baker came in from the rain, and was in the doorway when Calumet Red started out of the bunkhouse. He met Baker right there and his face was straight and bad and his nostrils swelled and without a word he dropped his head and hit Baker twice in the stomach and knocked Baker out of the door, down into the gray liquid mud of the grade.

The wind came back to him when he stood up, the mud slid in loose fragments all along his clothes; he walked in against the kid waiting at the doorway. The kid hit at him and missed, and Baker just walked in solid and slow and drove the kid backward, through the narrow aisle between the bunks, back into the rear space by the stove. The bunkhouse was full of men; they stood up to get out of the way, they rolled into the bunks to get out of the way. Calumet Red crouched and jumped at Baker, strong as a young ox and hurt Baker badly with his fists; but Baker moved on against him. He caught the kid's arms and tied them up and drove the kid against the shanty wall. He battered the kid's head against the wall and let go with his fists, smashing the kid's face, side to side; he caught him again and got his big arms around the kid's throat and shook him like a sack of straw, and hit him once more and dropped him. He felt mean enough at the moment to kill the boy and was ashamed of the feeling.

The only sound in the bunkhouse was the draw of the kid's breathing and his own. The kid was down in a corner; he looked up at Baker with his face bleeding and a dead, confused, hating color in his eyes.

Baker said: "Get up and sit in that chair, son."

The kid just sat there until Baker added, in the soft voice that never left him, "Do as I say, boy, or I'll break your neck." Calumet Red came off his haunches; he sat in the chair, his thick shoulders bunched over, his feet touching a stove poker lying on the floor. His glance reached the stove poker and rose swiftly, livened by a thought.

"Where you come from?" said Baker.

"Duluth," said the kid. "What of it?"

"Where's your dad?"

"In the pen, if he's alive," said the kid. "I dunno. I pulled out long time ago."

"Got a mother?"

"How the hell do I know?"

The kid's glance dropped to the poker and Tom Baker knew what was in his mind at once. Before the kid moved he brought his tough hand around like the sweep of an ax, palm open, and hit the kid on the side of the face. It was like the sound of an exploding bottle; the kid fell off the chair — he was thrown off — and struck the floor in a round heap. The kid was dirty all the way through, which was the way he had been taught by his kind of life. But maybe there was something below that was worth looking at; and then Baker knew there wasn't. For the kid brought up his hand to shield his face, and on his face was nothing but the cringing look of a whipped pup. No hatred, no life, no anger.

"I'm sorry for that, son," said Baker. "I shouldn't of done it."

Next morning the kid was gone. He had rolled his blankets and pulled out. But, driving team through the bottomless mud, with the rain slashing against him, Baker remembered what the kid had said about his people. His people had not been good and the kid had grown up without help. This was what happened when you left a boy alone in that mighty short space of childhood; when you didn't stand by to steady him and speak to him, and show him the proper road. This was what happened. When he thought of it — and he thought of it all that day — something faltered in him and fear got in him for the time he had been away from home. This was Friday. Saturday morning, driving past the line of shacks he saw Mr. Cochran come from the cookshack, wheel slowly and fall into the mud.

Baker wrapped the reins around the brake handle and got down and lifted Mr. Cochran out of the mud. Mr. Cochran was drunk; his legs would not hold him and Baker had to support him and push him back into the cookshack. He settled Mr. Cochran down on a bench. Mr. Cochran hooked his elbows against the long table and stared at Baker.

"You're all right — you're all right," he said. "You're all right."

Baker said in his slow, quiet way, "What's the need of getting drunk, Mr. Cochran? For a hunky, maybe. Not for you."

"Not for me?" mimicked Mr. Cochran. He was laughing. It was a giggling rush in his throat. He almost cried when he laughed. "Well, you're all right. Not for me, uh?" And then he quit laughing and it hurt Tom Baker to see what he saw. Mr. Cochran's face was pale and it was empty. You looked at it and you saw maybe misery, or foolishness, or maybe something behind that really was like the beginning of a black hole. But you didn't see any happiness or anything solid, such as a man with knowledge, like Mr. Cochran's knowledge, ought to have. All Mr. Cochran's knowledge wasn't enough; not enough to satisfy him or hold him together. So he walked out of a door, dead drunk, and fell in the mud.

It occurred to Tom Baker that it wasn't seemly for him to stand here spying on another man like that. So he said, "Mighty sorry, Mr. Cochran," and went back to his wagon. He drove down the grade, delivered his load and took the team to the barn; he didn't bother about noon meal, but rolled his blankets and got his time from the timekeeper, and headed home.

The day was over with early, drowned out by the rain fog. Passing Prairie, he supposed it would save a trip if he went into town and cashed his time slip, but haste was on him, as though he had wasted too much time away from home now. This mist kept rolling up against him until it got through his clothes and into his shoes; until he was solidly adrip. Deep in the darkness he heard

Delzell's dog barking a quarter mile back from the road. At the top of the dip he caught the shining of his own houselight — a little splinter of warmth that came out and touched him and quickened his heavy legs. It was ten o'clock. When he came up to the porch, his boots making a racket, the door opened and his wife stood there and the warmth of the room eddied against him.

She said, so calmly: "Better leave the blanket roll out there, Tom. Probably it's lousy."

He threw down the blanket roll, stepping into the room. Water began to collect at his feet, the pool gathering mud. He bent down to unlace his shoes, but the slight pressure of her arm drew him upright and she looked straight at him, at his eyes, and then she was smiling. "A long time, wasn't it, Tom?"

"Mighty long time."

"You're a funny man. You don't take to worry often. But when you do you worry hard. There never was anything to worry about. The children are all right. They'll always be all right — because of the kind of children they are. And because, maybe, of us."

"Well," he said, in slow, complete conviction, "I know that now." He moved out and got the boiler and filled it and hoisted it to the stove; and brought in the tub. He stood by the stove, shelling off his outer clothes, and watched his wife move around, making up a supper. His woolen underwear began to steam and to itch, and then he went up the stairs, and closed the attic window against the inbeating rain. Little Bill slept with his arms flung out and all his muscles loose. Lissie turned in her bed and smiled in sleep and brought up a hand, laying it against her face. Her body was a round ball beneath the quilts. When he came to Elzie's bed and saw the boy's tanned sober face he had a moment's tremendous regret for the three weeks spent away. Elzie's dark hair stuck up like straw sticks; he was getting long and thin from growth and there was a boy's smell on him. Baker stood there a little while, everything pretty clear in his mind. It took a good deal to make a man, and learning was only one of the things. The thing was, you had to stay by your children and show them how it all went, insofar as you knew. Maybe a word now and then, just a word; and a good deal of example, by the way you did a thing or didn't do it; but mostly by just living with them, so that everything sank in. So that when they grew up — if they had good blood and saw things straight they were all right. So that when they went away, they could look back and remember; and never go far wrong, because of what they remembered.

He went down and poured his water and had his bath, his wife laughing at the figure he made, and sat up to the table full of hunger. Afterwards he built a smoke in his pipe and sat by the stove, listening to the rain beat over his house, catching the raw freshness of the little currents of air drifting in. The sky would be washed clean and when the sun came again the land would be like new. Presently it was time for bed. He walked around the house, trying the windows, and wound the clock. Lying in bed, beside the warmth and the closeness of his wife, he had a tremendous feeling of happiness; everything went off his mind and he laughed silently at himself.

He said: "When the sun comes out again I think we'll just pack up the wagon and tent and go up in the hills. Maybe next week. Should be fine fishing in the lake. And I can show Little Bill the beavers. He ain't seen a beaver yet. We'll have a vacation. Next week."

Her voice was alive, amused; there was something in it to hit a man pretty hard. "That's next week, Tom."

"Sure. I know. And this is now."

Custom of the Country

People who had lived so closely together during the long crossing of the plains were scarcely the kind to fear their neighbors; and therefore not one of Portland's dozen houses had a lock. Nor was it the custom to knock on a door before entering; the habits of the trail were still strong in these settlers. At the Lord cabin, Rose Ann Talbot simply called out, "Here's your milk, Mrs. Lord," lifted the latch and walked into the cabin's single room.

A fireplace blaze lightened the afternoon grayness of the room and touched Hobart Walling, that bold and strutting little farmer who was here to drive his bargain. He had driven his stock in from the Tualatin, the mud of which was still on his boots and trousers; his face was roughened and crimsoned by weather and his close-set eyes held an aggressive shrewdness.

Dislike moved through Rose Ann as his glance touched her, ran across her cheeks with its prying familiarity, and returned to Lord. "You and your woman understand the work a farmer's wife has got to do. I wouldn't want Sarah to think it was an easy life."

Lord said, "Sarah's fourteen, and work's all she's done. That's all this family knows, is work. Hell, my woman was twelve when she married me."

Mrs. Lord stood near the fire, silent, apparently agreeable. Sarah, the main party to this dickering, remained in the shadows of the room's corner. She had a plain sweet face touched with freckles, and a flat body; her silence reflected the uncertainty of any immature little girl. There was nothing about her, Rose Ann thought, to show she really understood this bargaining or to show that she had any deep feeling about it. She was still; she was intent; she watched Hobart Walling closely.

"You'll get an extra half section of land with a wife," said Lord. "That's important, Hobart."

Walling nodded and glanced at Sarah. He said, "What you think about it, Sarah?"

"Yes."

"Well," said Walling, "then it's settled. I got to get back to the farm by Sunday night."

Lord said, "We'll fix it for Sunday morning. You talk to that Congregational preacher about it, Hobart."

Walling used the back of his hand to

scratch the whiskers Under his chin. He nodded at Sarah but he spoke to Mrs. Lord. "She got clothes and things? We won't get into town much this winter. I don't mind if you want to buy a few things for her on my account." He looked at Rose Ann again, and the greasy sensation renewed itself within her; then he turned out of the room.

Lord turned to his wife with sharp triumph: "That's it."

Mrs. Lord looked toward Sarah. "Sarah, you got a good practical man. You'll have a better home than I ever had."

Rose Ann tried to keep the protest out of her voice: "Sarah, do you really want to get married?"

She caught Mrs. Lord's wondering glance, and the annoyance on Lord's cheeks. Sarah's expression was one of smooth and flattered self-satisfaction. Her eyes were round and large. She was confident; she had had her own moment of triumph. "I'll be married — I won't be an old maid. I'll have a house. I'll have babies."

Rose Ann turned to leave the cabin before unwise words escaped her. Mrs. Lord called, "I'm grateful for the milk, Rose Ann," but she paid no attention. She walked along a slick pathway winding around the stumps of a future street, through the early twilight which came upon this settlement crouched between the river and the huge fir forest directly behind; she walked with her head down and her thoughts were fretful. The Lord family got a prosperous son-in-law to lean on while Walling took a hired girl without pay; for Sarah it was nothing but a doll-house dream magnified.

Entering her own cabin, Rose Ann lighted the candles and dished the meal and waited for her father to return from the store; there was distress in her face, and her father noticed it. "We must be out of salt or flour or something," he said.

"The Lords have just horse-traded Sarah to Walling."

The news didn't disturb him. "That's been coming."

"A fourteen-year-old girl marrying a man of thirty — a child marrying an old man."

"She's old enough," he said. "It's not uncommon. As for Walling, if he's an old man at thirty, what am I?" He sat up to the table ready to enjoy his meal. She took her place across from him, astonished that such a thing made no impression on him.

She said, "Would you have wanted me to be married at fourteen?"

"That's a different thing. You've had some education. The man you marry will

129

have some education. You'll want somebody who'll get on in the community, who'll wash his face before he comes to supper, who'll pull back your chair for you. But Sarah's not got those prospects. She's out of the Missouri backwoods. Not one of her ancestors ever learning to read or write; not one of them ever rising to a house made out of boards. This marriage will be the best ever made in her family. She'll be a thousand times better off than her people, and her children will get a chance she never had."

"She'll be a drudge," said Rose Ann — "and worn out at twenty."

Her father, usually so quick with his sympathies, sat back to give her his smiling tolerance. "We've all got to work and wear out — Sarah in one thing, you in another." Then, still smiling, he added, "Sarah, marrying at fourteen, is the common thing. You, single at twenty, are the exception."

She wondered how much he worried about her singleness, and from that she began to think of herself, for a little while forgetting Sarah. She rose to do the dishes, and a slight fear came to her because she was growing old and no man had yet appealed to her, though men had looked upon her and would have asked if she had encouraged them. Her father went to his rocker, slowly swaying it across the squeaky board on the floor. Sarah came back to Rose Ann's mind and when she had finished the dishes she left the house and walked along the pathway toward the riverbank.

A big bonfire burned close by Hawley MacBride's saw pits. As she came nearer she saw him standing on a log, trimming it with a broadax into a square timber to be used in somebody's building. By day, with a hired man, he stood at one of the pits and sawed out the boards which furnished such lumber as this town had; by night, with his hired man gone, he lighted his fire and worked late on timbers. The swinging of the ax was like him, unhurried, regular and patient; he was young and quietly stubborn in his persistent laboring.

Having her thoughts on Sarah, she went by him without speaking. Children were shouting through the shadows, to remind her that Sarah, passing from the drudgery of the Lord house to the drudgery of Walling's house, missed this fun which was hers by right of childhood. No youth for her, no running through shadows, no free girlhood, no knowing ever what it was like to have the eyes of a young man come to her with a message, no dreaming, no foolishness —

nothing but being old forever.

Mist came down upon the river, raw and strong, and water lapped against the muddy bluff at her feet. Hawley MacBride's ax ceased its metal ringing and in a moment she heard him whetting the edge of the blade with a stone. She turned to the fire and watched him make a few tentative strokes to test the sharpness of the ax, each light stroke rolling thin shavings from the log. He put the ax aside, lighted his pipe and sat down on the timber for a little talk, his smile coming across the fire. Black hair, with a single rolling curl to it that any woman might envy, dropped against his forehead.

"Do you know Sarah's going to marry Walling?" she asked. "It's a shameful thing."

He puttered at his pipe, clearly trying to understand what she meant. By the firelight his face cast off a bronze shadowing, his lips made a long roll, his eyes flashed against the blaze. He shook his head. "Guess she doesn't think so, or her people."

He was like her father; he could not see what she saw. She stood still and for a moment wondered if she were wrong; but the distaste would not die. "She's a little girl, anxious to be a woman. This flatters her. She doesn't really know what it means. Of course her folks would like to see her married. They're poor and Walling's got land and money."

"It's their affair. Not yours and mine."

She said, "It's like a Siwash Indian selling his daughter for a string of beads."

He watched her with a sobering, steady attention, slowly drawing on his pipe, his big hands idle across his knees. "Maybe," he said. "But it won't do to interfere."

"You'd interfere if you saw a man trying to kill another man, wouldn't you?"

He brushed that remark aside with instant common sense. "Not the same. No man consents to being killed. But Sarah's consented to be married."

"The kind of consent you can buy with a bag of candy. She doesn't know."

He rose from the timber and tapped out the smoke from his pipe. He put his hands behind his back and looked into the fire, challenged by what she had said. He brought up his glance, not with the expression he had worn before, but with a direct interest in her. "It troubles you, doesn't it?"

She said, "If Lord had a job, maybe he'd think better of letting her get married."

"That's just hoping," he said.

"It's got to be stopped."

"People live their own way. Maybe it's not

133

such a good way but it's theirs and that's their business."

She was distressed that he wouldn't see, and instinct to protect Sarah grew stronger. "She's got the right to grow up and be free a while before she turns into Walling's slavey. She's got the right to have a man look at her with something nice in his eyes. I can't bear to think of this marriage. It's indecent."

"It does trouble you," he said.

"It does," she said, and turned away. Half the distance toward her cabin she looked behind, not hearing his ax resume its chopping; he stood at the fire with his hands still behind him, the firelight making his large shoulders larger. He was a high, impressive shape against the darkness; he was a block of solidness reassuring to look upon, and she looked upon him a long moment before continuing her way homeward.

MacBride's fire lost its yellow glow and became a dull redness against the earth; he had a notion to go on working, but the thought wasn't good and he turned toward Billy Ashford's hut at the far end of the settlement.

Half a dozen men were in the place when he arrived, other bachelors gathered for a little talk before the day was done, and Rose Ann's father and Hobart Walling. A jug of blue ruin stood on the table with a few tin cups. MacBride poured and drank his tot, stood a moment to get the hang of the conversation and sat down in the corner, wedging his shoulders between two other men.

He let the talk roll around him, while he gave some thought to Hobart Walling. The man's short body carried considerable power in it, heavy muscles with short spans to them; he had a flushed face slightly marked by smallpox, and there were pale scars on the high edge of his forehead, no doubt from the rough-and-tumble fights in the past. He was an energetic creature; even now his vitality made him restless. He said to Billy Ashford, "How much you pay for this liquor?"

"Couple dollars a gallon."

"Well, it's not bad."

"Hell," said Ashford, "it's terrible. I'm surprised at your judgment."

"A drink's a drink," said Walling.

The talk turned to cougars in the hills behind the town. It swung from cougars to food, and from food to the coming of Christmas. MacBride hung his hands over his doubled knees and idly massaged his knuckles. The drink did him good. He dropped his head and closed his eyes, listening to Walling's voice.

Billy Ashford said, "Hear you're going to get married, Hobart."

"Sunday."

"I'll be glad when a few more women get into this country," said Ashford.

"You can pick up a good squaw any time," said Walling.

There was a small silence, which Ashford presently filled with his most casual question: "You had one a couple years ago. What happened to her?"

"Oh," said Walling, putting it aside as a thing of no consequence, "I sent her back to her people."

MacBride opened his eyes and gave Walling a closer glance. The silence went on, and Walling, feeling it, stared around the group. His eyes closed down somewhat. He said briefly, "Nothing unusual about it. A lot of men have done it." His glance stopped on MacBride and he said, with a lift to his tone, "What's wrong about it?"

"I hadn't said," replied MacBride.

"Well, then, let's not discuss it."

"I'm not," said MacBride. He got up from his crowded corner. "Billy, it was a good drink. When that jug runs out, I'll buy the next gallon." He took time to fill and light his pipe at the candle, the light dancing against his eyes, making them sparkle; and then he ducked his head beneath the low doorway and left Ashford's. He went on slowly, mouth puckered around the pipe stem, his head down and his hands behind him. At the fork of the pathway he paused a moment and then he turned toward the Lord cabin.

After breakfast, with the house swept, Rose Ann took her bucket down the trail to a small meadow beyond the settlement and milked the cow. A third of the milk she poured into skim pans and set them out to cool on the covered shelf; the rest of it she divided into three small buckets, one for the Ballards, one for the Snows, one for the Lords. These were the latest arrivals in the settlement and therefore the poorest. Setting out to deliver the pails, she looked toward the river and saw MacBride already working at the saw pits. He stood above a log on one of the pits, guiding a long crosscut through the log while some man, not seen by her, stood down in the pit beneath the log at the other end of the saw. She noticed that there was a crew at the second pit this morning; he had found extra workers.

She delivered her last pail to Mrs. Lord,

who was working up bread, surrounded by five of her younger children. "I don't know what I'd do without milk, Rose Ann. It's good to have neighbors. Lord's working now. Hawley MacBride hired him for the saw pit. Now then, if his health don't break down —"

"What's the matter with his health?" asked Rose Ann.

"Always been a frail man, strong as he looks. His energy just runs out."

Rose Ann walked to the doorway and looked across the clearing to Hawley Mac-Bride on the saw-pit log. Her eyelids almost touched as she watched his body swinging up and down with the saw, and her mouth softened. She spoke over her shoulder: "Now that he's working, maybe you won't want Sarah to be married so young."

"What's that got to do with it?" asked Mrs. Lord in surprise. "She's got a fine chance."

Rose Ann turned about. "Mrs. Lord, is Sarah in love with him?"

Mrs. Lord straightened from her chore and laid a hand against her side to contain some brief twitch of pain. She was not so dull and indifferent as she seemed, Rose Ann decided; her face became strong and wide-awake. "That will do for thinkin', but we got to be practical. Maybe your father can support you while you do your dreamin'. We're too poor for that. Sarah's got to do the best she can."

Rose Ann dropped her glance, embarrassed at the expression on Mrs. Lord's face. Sarah was bent over a washtub in the yard, her straw-colored hair coming down over a face freckled and pointed and plain. Rose Ann went over. Sarah's hands were red and her bones were poorly clad with flesh; she needed so much time to fill herself with things which would glow out of her and stain her features with maturity. It was hard to know much about a girl of fourteen — where the child left off and the woman began. Rose Ann tried to remember back to when she was fourteen, but she couldn't quite revive that time. She said, "Sarah — what will you call him? Hobart?"

Sarah said, "Oh, no. That would be like calling my father by his first name. I'll call him Mr. Walling."

Rose Ann went back home to cut up a piece of beef and put it into the big iron pot. She peeled her potatoes and onions to go into the stew later; she cleaned the churn and poured into it the accumulated cream, and sat on a chair with the churn between her knees, operating the dasher up and down with a vigorous, steady stroke. She couldn't get Sarah out of her mind. It was so strange to her that she stood alone, that nobody else saw it as she saw it. Was she a queer old maid?

She thought about that and then she remembered that Hawley MacBride had hired Lord and she thought with some surprise: Why, I did make him understand a little bit.

She turned the butter and spent half an hour kneading it. She added the vegetables to the stew and finished off the butter into pretty bricks stamped with an oak leaf. She had dinner ready for her father when he came in at noon, and later washed the dishes and straightened the house again. The afternoon came, and she stood at the window, watching the people of the settlement move around at their various chores. She saw the gray clouds rolling over the sky and the dull afternoon's glitter on the wet green trees; she saw Hobart Walling come up from the river and go into Lord's — and very suddenly she hated the man with a great intensity. She got her light shawl and walked directly to Mrs. Ellenwood's.

Mrs. Ellenwood was a gentlewoman who had followed a restless husband out of a comfortable New York home to this land of mud and dust. She had made the best of it. The two rooms of her small frame house were wonderfully peaceful with their rag rugs, with the rose dishes so carefully brought over the plains, and with the snow-white curtains and waxed maple chairs. She was a tall woman, still pretty at forty, and her charm made Rose Ann feel quite young. Mrs. Ellenwood occupied a rocker in her afternoon hour of leisure and knitting. She might have been a great lady in a mansion, for that was the air of the room at this moment. "Take a chair, Rose Ann."

"I'm out of the notion to be peaceful. It's Sarah that troubles me."

Mrs. Ellenwood considered Rose Ann. "You have got a very firm look on your face. I have been trying to think of a useful wedding gift for Sarah. She needs so much to start with."

"It's wrong," said Rose Ann. "Don't you think it is?"

"The girl seems to want to do it."

"To a man more than twice as old. She oughtn't think of any marriage yet."

"Well, many women have married that early — some to old men and some to men they couldn't rightly say they loved. I do observe most of these marriages turn out well."

"No," said Rose Ann, disappointed in this woman she so greatly admired. "I can't believe it. It's wrong."

Mrs. Ellenwood fell silent, and looked through the window, gentle regret on her face. She gave Rose Ann a faint smile. "It's because you can dream. There are so many girls who can't dream. They take a man and make the best of it. That's Sarah. Suppose you talked her out of it. It would be another man next year — maybe one not so well provided. What have you done to her then? I wouldn't risk changing her life. She's plain, she's poor, she's never known anything but work and dirt. She wouldn't even understand what you're talking about."

"She needs a chance to know," said Rose Ann. "She should go to school and grow up. Then she can choose a man."

"How will she get a chance to do this? Her parents won't do it for her."

"I will," said Rose Ann. "I'll take her in and raise her."

Mrs. Ellenwood shook her head. "You do surprise me. But, Rose Ann, you can't talk Lord or his wife out of a son-in-law with money." She paused, she had something further to say and hesitated to say it. "You know, Rose Ann, that men run the world. You're a girl and you've got no power to change men's minds."

"But," said Rose Ann, "a man might help me."

Curiosity was a clear thing on Mrs. Ellenwood's face. "I didn't know any man interested you."

"I didn't say that," answered Rose Ann swiftly.

A fugitive humor ran along Mrs. Ellenwood's mouth and was at once suppressed. She said something that was in contradiction with what she had said before.

"Well, Rose Ann, maybe we're so close to the earth we don't see the sky. Life's very hard in a new country and people get coarse sometimes. If it's in your heart to help Sarah, then you've got to do it."

"That helps me," said Rose Ann, and left the house.

She stood a moment outside Mrs. Ellenwood's door. The ringing of the woodchoppers' axes came from the timber, and the "swash-swash" of Hawley MacBride's saw was an unbroken rhythm. Not many men cared to work with him at the saw pits, for few of them could stand that kind of labor. Her eyes narrowed on him, watching his body grow stiff and broad-shouldered when he straightened. A group of men stood over by Kerr's store, and another man came sauntering along to join them — Hobart Walling. Presently the three went into the store.

She looked again toward MacBride, and drew a long breath, her heart beating fast. She thought: "I have got to do it," and went toward the store with dread in her. It was a hard thing to pass through the door. She stopped before it with a feeling of weakness. She looked through the door, seeing Walling and the two men lounging before the counter. Kerr was behind the counter — and all of them were laughing at some joke. She stepped inside. They quit talking, Kerr giving the others a short warning with his hand. The talk hadn't been meant for her ears, she understood. She went on to the counter.

"I should like a spool of thread — black thread."

The silence of the men was one of those amused, indifferent silences; they were waiting for her to be done with her buying and go. She felt Walling's eyes watching her and she turned her head quickly and caught the sliding, pushing quality of his glance. It didn't drop; it drove boldly at her.

She said, "What are you staring at, Mr. Walling? Is a woman strange to you?"

He straightened. "That's no way to talk to a man."

"You're very brave," she said. "That is, before women."

He showed her a deepening color. He looked at the other men and back at her. "I've not bothered you," he said shortly. "Go home where you belong and don't try to break into men's talk."

"You," she said, "are a fat lunk of a creature. Do you ever shave or ever wash? You smell like a barn. And here you are, telling me what I ought to do. I shall stay here. You do the going."

"If I were your father," he said, "I'd teach you your place."

"You have not that intelligence, Mr. Walling."

Her remark humiliated him before an audience. His instant and unthinking prejudice flared. "By God, get back to your place before I take you for another kind of a woman."

She hit him across the face with her hand. He raised his hand and reached for her, but she stepped aside and hit him again. She turned swiftly, remembering a stack of ax handles by the door. She seized one and came back toward him. "Now, then," she said, "do you mean to lay that grimy paw on me, Mr. Walling?"

He would have done so had not the store-keeper suddenly said, "That will be all, Walling."

Walling checked himself and gave Rose Ann a killing glance. He said, "I must take this up with your father. I shall not accept it."

"If you step into our cabin," she said, "I'll shoot you."

He checked himself quite suddenly; he changed his feelings in remarkably fast time. "Now," he said in a complaining voice, "who brought this on anyhow?" Then he gave the men around him a shake of his head, carefully circled Rose Ann and left the store.

She had not only offended Hobart Walling, she noticed; she had also offended Mr. Kerr and the other two men. All men stuck together — they said nothing but they created an air that was thick with disapproval. She picked up her thread, murmuring, "That will be all, Mr. Kerr," and left the store. Her knees were trembling and she felt mildly giddy.

She got supper, lighted the candles and turned to the doorway to wait for her father to turn the trail which came out of the lower part of town. When he swung into sight she noticed that he walked faster than usual. He saw her at the door and quickened his pace; he came on, staring at her with a tight, strict expression on his face. He went directly through the back way to wash up. She dished up and took her seat, knowing that he knew, but she said nothing when he took his place at the table. He helped himself to the meat, took one taste of it, and laid down his fork.

"Now, then," he said, "what did you say to Walling? Were you interfering in his affairs?"

"He was impolite. I slapped his face. Try the greens. I fixed them with grandmother's sauce."

"Rose Ann," said her father, "did you threaten him with a gun if he came around here?"

"Oh, yes," said Rose Ann.

"My God, that's for me to do, not for you. Now I shall have to demand an apology from him. You're certain —"

The door was still open, with somebody standing in it. Talbot lifted his glance, taking care to erase the fretfulness he had displayed. He said cheerfully, "Come in, Hawley."

Rose Ann sat quite still, startled; she didn't look around until Hawley MacBride spoke to her. "Rose Ann," he said, "did you say anything to Walling about Sarah?"

She said, "I do wonder at all this excitement. No. He was impolite and I slapped him. Now that I think of it, I wish I'd slapped him again."

"Dammit," said Talbot, "you ought not become publicly involved with a man."

"Then," said Hawley MacBride, "he looked wrong at you and was impolite when you mentioned it?"

"That's what it was," said Rose Ann. "Is there a law which stops a woman from protecting herself against a man?"

Hawley MacBride said, "Maybe there ought to be a law protecting a man from a woman," and left the cabin.

"Rose Ann," complained her father, "I've got to go do a disagreeable job directly after supper. You ought to bear that in mind when you fight a man. Some other man has got to take care of it."

"Enjoy your supper first," said Rose Ann . . .

Last seen, Hobart Walling bad been traveling in the direction of Billy Ashford's cabin; and that was where MacBride found him, sitting on a corner box in the little place while Ashford threw together some kind of supper. He was crouched over with his pipe, a good drink of blue ruin giving him cheer and appetite; he looked up with a lively attention when MacBride stepped into the cabin, and noted the gray sparkling in MacBride's eyes. He laid his pipe carefully aside and rose from the box. He looked around him for elbow room; he squared himself. MacBride stepped across the room, lifting both arms, nodding his warning at the other man. Walling grumbled, "The hell with you," and swung out with his fists.

"Get out of my cabin to do that!" shouted Ashford.

He ducked, put one foot in the fireplace, and clawed his way aside from the two stamping men. Hawley MacBride knocked down Walling's arms. He missed a blow and hit Walling with his chest. He threw out his hand and took Walling under the chin, snapping back the man's neck. Walling seized the table and tried to lift it, but MacBride tore it out of his hands and flung it aside, tin dishes, crockery jug and utensils and all coming down as a jangling rain on the floor. Walling laid his back against the cabin wall and punched. He lifted his booted leg and rammed it outward. MacBride shifted his narrow hips, came in and struck Walling on the chin. Walling rolled his head and slid to the floor.

"Damned long time messing around with it," said MacBride.

Ashford came back into the cabin, cursing both of them. "It's a hell of a way to treat a man."

"Certainly is," said MacBride. "But this is private, and we won't need to say much about it."

"The hell I won't."

MacBride turned a thoughtful eye on Ashford. "No, Billy — just don't."

"All right — all right," said Ashford.

Walling got up from the floor and put both hands across his face as though he were washing away the fog.

"Hobart," said MacBride, "if you talk rough to one woman, you might talk rough to another. Just begin to walk — and don't stop at the Lords' on your way. If you make another stab to marry Sarah, or if you tell anybody why you changed your mind, I'll just come find you and lick hell right out of you."

Walling said in a jaded wonder, "What started all this? My God, I never did anything."

MacBride grinned. "You just ran into opposition." He left the cabin, the grin breaking into one small chuckle as he turned homeward.

Rose Ann did the dishes while her father left to discharge his dismal chore. He soon returned with the news, astonished by Mac-Bride's act. He was, Rose Ann observed, relieved that he had not had to call Hobart Walling to account, yet he was also piqued that another man had taken the duty from him. "What's MacBride got to do with this?"

Rose Ann smiled, "I couldn't say."

She unpinned her apron and gave herself a glance in the mirror. She touched up her hair, she studied her face, she straightened her shoulders. As she left the house, she dropped a new notion behind her: "The Lords are very poor. They need help. I want Sarah to stay with us and go to school." She went out of the door before her father had time to answer. It was always better to let men think about things awhile.

MacBride's bonfire burned against the sooty shadows and he stood on another log, chipping it into a timber with his ax. He had his pipe in his mouth and by the yellowing light his face looked forbidding. He showed no scars from the fight She paused beside the blaze, well knowing that he was aware of her presence even though he ignored her and went on with that precise, light ax work. She spread her hands before the fire and was content; he would be thinking of what he wanted to say to her.

He reached the end of the log and straightened. He looked at her. He gave the ax a mighty swing and buried it in the log and stepped down. He filled his pipe and got a coal to light it. He stood across the fire, giving her the full fretful weight of his glance.

"Woman," he said, "you just naturally played hell to have your way. You took advantage of Walling to get into a quarrel. You got insulted deliberately and you used me to pay off the insult, and now you've got the marriage killed, as you wanted."

She said, "You told him to leave Sarah alone?"

His answer came out slowly: "I told him."

"Do you think he'll mind you, Hawley?"

"He'll mind me."

"That's nice," she said, and showed him her pleased relief.

He shook his head, shocked by the implications of her act. "It was a fine piece of scheming," he said, "and no doubt you now know you can put a man at your mercy any time you please. Great stars, if you're going to be a meddling woman you can have everybody in this settlement shootin' at one another. It won't do, Rose Ann, and I'll not have it."

"It was wicked," she agreed. "I shan't do it again, unless my spirit just boils over."

"Why," he asked, "did you pick on me to do your fighting?"

"Because," she said, pleasantly matter-of-fact with her answer, "you're the only one who can whip him."

He frowned at her. "Don't do it again." She met the frown with her agreeable expression; she folded her hands before her. He watched her and he lost his soberness. "Well," he said, "I can't say I didn't enjoy the chance to rough him. The man's a hog. But we can't be doing that all the time, Rose Ann. It's no way to get along."

"No," she said, "it isn't. We only do that when people won't take care of meanness any other way." She made a little gesture; she spoke with a quiet intensity: "What's strength for if not to use to make things right? And this just wasn't right. It's nice you hired Lord."

"Lord," he said, "is no good. He won't work. A man's entitled to a chance, but no man's entitled to loaf while others feed him. It's not charity to support a man who's able to support himself."

"Well," she said, "you gave him the chance. I'm going to take Sarah into my house. She'll come, and the Lords will be willing. Now she'll get the chance to grow, and she'll have time to find a man that looks at her in the right way."

He watched her with an attention so close that she finally lowered her glance to the fire. He said, "Maybe we get too rough around here; maybe we forget how things ought to be. It's a settlement full of men, and men do get careless in the way they live. I've thought about that."

Suddenly she put a hand to her mouth. "Lordy, I clean forgot to milk the cow tonight." She turned from the fire, but she paused a moment in seeming thought. It was a suggestive pause, which worked well. Hawley MacBride reached for a coal to relight his pipe and turned carelessly toward her.

"I'll walk over there with you."

"I wouldn't want to stop you from your work."

"I have thought about that lately, too. I work enough. It has occurred to me that solitary work is like solitary drinking. It's not good."

She said, in her nicest tone, "Well, it's something to think about, I suppose," and went with him along the trail. Somewhere in the misting night a cowbell sent out its lengthened and subdued strokes of sound.

Good Marriage

At evenfall this Saturday, with supper done and the soft sweet-smelling shadows of summer drifting against the prairie like gray gauze, neighbors began to come in. The Hurds were the original homesteaders on the Silver Bow's south rim, having settled this quarter section at a time when the cattlemen still made it dangerous for a nester, and so it was natural that the Hurd house should be more or less a gathering point. In any event Sam Hurd, who loved a sociable evening and loud argument better than most men, usually had a keg of beer cooling in the well and this was a powerful inducement to the lean, dry and clannish Missourian settlers — the Gants, the Lockyears, the Cobbetts and the Prillifews.

The children were all outside, running through the shadows, their quick-issued cries riding the night. Men sat around the room, chairs canted back against the wall, and the women were together at one end, now and then speaking among themselves, but always listening with half an ear to the talk of the men. Tobacco smoke laid its pall around them, so thick that the table lamp cast a mist-blue shadow; the smell of fried pork lingered in the house and the warmth of the day held on. Mrs. Prillifew's new baby began to cry; she unbuttoned the front of her dress and slid it down from one shoulder, uncovering her nipple to let the baby nurse; its small mouth made a steady, smacking sound.

Lisbeth Hurd moved over the room, straight and large-breasted and robust; at twenty she was the oldest of the Hurd children, pretty enough to bring the eyes of men around to her with a covert interest. She took Cobbett's empty glass, refilled it at the beer keg and passed it back to him; and stood by the beer keg, watching the men and indifferently listening. The sludge of Henry Zimmer's pipe began to fry. He reversed the bowl against his heavy hand, emptying it and refilling it. Henry Zimmer was one of the Hurds' two boarders. Bob Law, sitting long-legged in the doorway, was the other. Both these young men were building shanties on new quarter section claims across the deep canyon on the Silver Bow.

Lisbeth Hurd watched Henry Zimmer's square face glisten when the lighted match played across the pipe bowl; nothing hurried this man and nothing much moved him.

Talk broke around her, idle and cheerful, and slowly her glance turned to Bob Law in the doorway. Bob Law nursed a cigarette, his head dipped aside as though he listened to the night or saw pictures on the far prairie; the silhouette of his face was long and taciturn and sharp. Studying him, Lisbeth's expression was tight-caught by soberness, her eyes had a depthless dark in them, her shoulders moved faintly.

Sam Hurd, who never was able to speak in a tone less than a half-shout, said: "It don't do no good to grow a lot of fruit. A man's only got so much time and it don't make sense to waste it waterin' a lot of trees. You got to raise things in this country that can shift for themselves, or you break your back."

Henry Zimmer spoke up, dogmatic and calm. "I grow hay, when I get started. I grow hay and feed stock. I run a feeder ranch, like they do in Iowa. Maybe I try corn."

Sam Hurd listened approvingly. This young man was after his own tastes, thrifty and marked for success. Down the road they heard the steady clip-clop of a trotting horse, whereupon Sam Hurd said: "Who was that I heard goin' by here two o'clock the other morning in a rig?"

Cobbett answered: "Bill Shasto, bringin'

Nellie Grace home. Nellie told her old man they had trouble crossin' the ford."

Sam Hurd let out a great burst of laughter and all of these men were grinning, knowing Nellie Grace. Hurd said: "She better marry Shasto before the baby comes along."

"Like Pete Root's wife," offered Prillifew. "Pete still claims it ain't his boy."

"Whut should he care for?" countered Sam Hurd. "It's one more boy, for chores." He swiggled the beer around his glass, pleased with the smoke and the warmth and the comfort of neighbors; suddenly he reached forward with his broad hand and hit Lisbeth across the hips. "Lisbeth, there's a thought for you. Get your man to take you out in a buggy.'

Lisbeth turned her dark eyes on her father, unstirred and unembarrassed. "What man?"

"My God," said Hurd, "you got the choice of anybody on prairie."

Mrs. Hurd's voice was a steady tone on the edge of all this. "You parboil it fifteen minutes, change to a little fresh water and add the kraut." While she talked her eyes watched Lisbeth carefully, seeing Lisbeth's glance swing and stop on Bob Law at the doorway. "The flavor comes from not leavin' the kraut on the stove too long."

The clip-clop of hoofs died in the yard and an assured young man, sandy-haired and smiling and dressed in neat townsman's clothes, picked his way across Bob Law's outstretched legs. "I saw the lights and heard the noise and thought I'd say hello."

This was Cam Skelton, who owned the drygoods store in Prairie City; and since he was in a way foreign to the slack, comfortable homestead group, Sam Hurd accorded him the courtesy of rising. Mrs. Hurd left her chair, pleased and somewhat disturbed at his presence. "Lisbeth, get Mr. Skelton a glass of beer. You mustn't mind such an untidy house, Mr. Skelton."

"It is an attractive house, Mrs. Hurd," said Cam Skelton with his most gallant manners. He paid his respects to the women with an inclusive statement. "You homestead ladies are the finest housekeepers in the world."

"We eat well," admitted Sam Hurd. "Had supper?"

Lisbeth moved around Cam Skelton, drew a glass of beer, and offered it to him. He said, "Thanks, I've eaten, but the beer will be a pleasure after the ride." He saluted Lisbeth with the glass; over its rim his eyes held her — they were quick eyes, round and bright-colored. From the corner of the room

Mrs. Hurd watched this man, the way he looked at Lisbeth. Talk had ceased in front of the townsman but he finished his beer and brought the talk alive again in an easy way. "It has been a good year. No grasshoppers and no drouth. There's a new settlement going in below town, on the Sweet Fork. Time will come, Sam, when you settlers will have the cattlemen pushed back beyond the bench."

"Time will come," said Sam Hurd in his loud, positive voice, "when we'll pass the laws in this country, and by damn we'll scrunch them like they have been scrunchin' us."

"Thanks for the beer," said Cam Skelton. He paused a moment, cool enough to disregard the crowd while he put his glance on Lisbeth. There was a full interest in him; she saw it as she stood calmly before him, not showing expression. Presently he ducked his head at the group and left the house. Silence held on until the pacing of his horse softened in the distance. Then Sam Hurd said: "As for corn, Henry, the Ioway kind won't do out here. We got to get a seed that will stand dry weather. Well, it will come." Talk rose up again and the tobacco smoke blurred everything.

Lisbeth drew a glass of beer and moved

to the doorway. She stood there, looking down at Bob Law until his face lifted. She said, "Beer?" and watched him take it and look away. The top of his head was dye-black; there was a scar on his cheek, which was part of his past — from a horse or a man or from a woman. She didn't know. He was a cowpuncher who had ridden out of the hills to take up a quarter section and the way of his life had left him taciturn. He wasn't at all like the practical, heavy, loud-speaking homestead men. He was loose-jointed and narrow-hipped from riding; he was an easy swinging man but at times he moved with an astonishing swiftness; something was inside of him, hard and intense and strange. But it was well covered. The open front of his shirt showed the bronze-brown skin of his chest.

The Prillifew baby was again mewling and it was time for the settlers to leave. They went away, family by family in their rigs, the children's backward calling riding the moon-less night in undulating, long-sustained bars of sound. Bob Law had gone on to the corral. Idly following, Lisbeth put her shoulders to the corral bars, looking up at him. He didn't seem to see her; he stared into the black sweep of the prairie, he was listening to its vague voices and its silence. But she knew he was aware of her; it was something in the set of his body, in his stillness.

"Where'd you come from, Bob?"

"Off there," he said, pointing at the hills. He had the brief and flat tone of a man who didn't use his voice much. In the dark she saw his face come down to her and felt the sudden roughness of his eyes. He said, "Good night," moving away to the small tent at the edge of the corral. She watched the lantern light spring up; she watched his shadow turn and crook as he undressed and saw it stand straight for a moment. Then the light died and a little later she caught the thin smell of a cigarette; he would be lying on the cot, smoking in the dark.

Lisbeth returned to the house to catch up the beer glasses and straighten the chairs. The children had started to bed and Henry Zimmer had gone up to the spare room. She heard his boots hit the floor, one and then another, and the groaning of the bedsprings as he settled down. This would be all the sound from that room; he would sleep the night through, without motion, his heavy snoring making a steady echo through the house.

Sam Hurd said in a tone that was, for him, extremely mild: "Henry's a damned smart young Dutchman. There's your man, Lisbeth. He'll make a fine farm."

Mrs. Hurd said, "Ah," in a dissenting tone. She stood by the table, not speaking again until Sam Hurd slowly retreated to the corner bedroom. Afterwards she added: "Not him, Lisbeth. You've got plenty of choice. You make a good marriage. Look at me. I had no choice. I ain't sorry, I ain't complaining, but you got things different. You don't have to be a farmer's wife. You can choose. Why do you think Cam Skelton came here? You could live in town and drive your own rig. You could dress like those women do. You make a good marriage. You got the chance — just once you've got it."

In her room, beside the kitchen, Lisbeth undressed and got into her white nightgown and stood in the room's center, braiding back her hair. Her father's and mother's voices came from the corner of the house as a steady murmur, and died, and silence closed in. She blew out the lamp, opened the side door and stood in the velvet density of the night. There was a faint wind rising off the prairie; it ran softly along her body. When she leaned against the pump handle, its metal coolness was sharp against her breasts. From this porch she watched the black outline of Bob Law's tent, thinking intimately of him; and retreated to her room.

She stood in the yard, after breakfast, watching Law and Henry Zimmer saddle their horses. Henry had a solid plug, broad of beam and meant for the plow; it was an animal Law always looked upon with a faint show of irony, for his own pony was range bred and a little bit tricky on these fresh mornings, crowhopping around the dirt with Law sitting deep and careless in the saddle. When they passed down the trail into the Silver Bow canyon she noticed that Law had forgotten his lunch; but she didn't call him back. It was four miles across the canyon to where these two had their adjoining quarter sections; she would take the lunch to Law later. Back in the house she put the lunch on the side table and had her own breakfast with her mother and the smaller children.

Her mother said: "I want you to go to town. I need some long straight pins and five yards of gingham, red check, and a spool of white thread." She looked at her daughter carefully. "Wear your gray dress; it don't muss up in the sidesaddle." When Lisbeth was in the saddle and ready to go, her mother came out to give her two silver dollars and another critical survey. "You look well. You've got a way. Maybe it is a little bit like the way of women who don't live on farms. Be nice to him, Lisbeth. It is all you need to do."

Lisbeth said softly: "How nice?"

"A woman must think about these things. You want to make a good marriage. For some men, like Zimmer who is dumb, you can be forward. For some you can't. It is something you must find out for yourself, when you see what's on his face."

This was why she was being sent to town, Lisbeth knew; to be nice to Cam Skelton. The thread and gingham and pins were just extra. She went swinging down the road, with the blur of Prairie City in the distance. Dust rose behind her in a long pale diffused cloud, shutting out the view of the ranch. Across the Silver Bow canyon she saw the thin dots of two riders, which would be Law and Henry Zimmer splitting off to their claims. High on the southern ridge cattlemen raised dust with a driven herd and the sun was the bright half-hot sun of late September.

There were ways with men, as her mother had said. One way was Nellie Grace's way. For men like Shasto and Zimmer and many others, it was the quick and easy way to catch a man; but for Cam Skelton it would only shame her before him, for Skelton was a townsman with different thoughts. A woman could only hint, and not be common. These things Lisbeth Hurd knew; it was a knowledge that came out of some obscure place, to make her wise, to make her look upon the world with cool eyes. But then she thought of Bob Law and was not sure. For he was another kind of man; there was something in him, like a dream, like a picture. There were words for this but she did not know them, could not find them. He saw things in the sky, he felt things through the shadows that others did not.

Prairie City's street was a gray lane of dust between a long double row of stiff paintless buildings; wagons and horsemen moved along it as she passed on to the drygoods store, racked the horse and stepped into the cool twilight of Cam Skelton's store. She heard Skelton's voice before she saw him. It was the quick, rising voice of a pleased man. He came out of the rear shadows, his round eyes aware of her.

She said: "Some long pins, some white thread — and five yards of gingham, red checked pattern."

He had a light way with his talk. He said, "What's in you anyway, Lisbeth? I wish I knew." He touched her hand. "Be easier if I did."

"Checked pattern," she said and let her hand drop.

Afterwards, having bought these things, she waited for her change. This store was still and fragrant and empty. Cam Skelton's steps made queer softened echoes in it. She thought of her mother's advice with a distant interest, and watched Cam Skelton come back. He put the change in her hand, and took her hand. "If I brought a rig around tonight, Lisbeth, would you ride?"

"No-o," she said, "not tonight."

"Some night?"

"Some night," she said and made her small smile for him. She was a well-shaped girl, graceful even in this motionless attitude, with her mouth softened by the smile and her eyes meeting him coolly.

He said at once, "You don't need to run away from a man, Lisbeth," and brought his hands up. He touched her shoulders and then she felt his resolution and his sudden change of temper as he pulled her toward him. The brightness had gone out of his eyes; they were rough-gray and full of a thing clear to her. She didn't know why, but she struck his arms down and hit him in the chest and went by him, angry enough to kill him. He called in an irritated voice: "Wait," and she paused at the door and swung around. He came up to her, his pride stung. Suddenly he was a little man, small of wrist and shoulder, smelling of his own store; and in this critical, outraged light she looked at him, and spoke her mind. Across the street stood the saloon with its second-story windows showing green drawn shades — hiding the women who lived there She said: "If that's the way you feel, go over there — above the saloon."

He said: "That's a hell of a thing for a girl to say. I guess I judged you wrong. What did you come here for anyway? Just for eighty cents' worth of goods?"

She marched out, with the package under her arm, stepped to the sidesaddle and ran out of town, still angered. But halfway home she suddenly smiled to herself. It was nice to know she had a woman's attractiveness. It helped; it made her feel something she hadn't felt before. Maybe he was wrong about her — but maybe he wasn't. What was a woman? What was she when she looked at Bob Law and had her own warm thoughts? What was she when the wind blew its strong wild smells down from the benchlands and stirred her heart; when she walked through the dark earth's shadows and felt the strength of her body like a heavy weight? There was no sign of this on her face; she was an idle girl swinging to the pace of the horse, color soft on her cheeks and a stamped gravity in her eyes.

She stepped off in the yard before her mother, who said eagerly: "Maybe you asked him out to supper?"

"No," she said. "I never thought of that." She went by her mother, caught up Bob Law's lunch, and returned to the horse.

"Maybe he said he'd come to see you?" said Mrs. Hurd.

"No," said Lisbeth, "he never did," and trotted down the canyon trail.

From the height of the rim the river was an urgent, winding streak far below, held in by the gray and yellow canyon walls; at the bottom of the canyon she crossed a shallow gravel ford, passed through a little cluster of willows and rose slowly to the south rim. Before her lay the sage-covered flats, running far to the empty north, directly ahead stood Henry Zimmer's fresh homestead shanty, its raw boards yellow in the sunlight; a half mile to the left stood Bob Law's house. Threading the sage as she went that way, she flushed slow-hopping jack rabbits from covert. Coming nearer she saw the pile of dirt mounded near the house, which was from the well he was digging. At intervals he appeared from the well, hauled up a bucket of dirt, dumped it, and disappeared in the well again.

She turned the horse over to the well and sat in the saddle, watching. He was twenty feet down, loosening the soil with a short-handled pick and dumping it into the bucket; he had a ladder rigged against the well wall, and when the bucket was full, he climbed out and windlassed up the bucket; it was the hard way of digging a well — and a little bit dangerous at this depth.

She said: "You forgot your lunch."

He said: "I guess I never gave it a thought. Thanks." He came over and took the lunch. He was stripped to the waist, his trouser belt pinched against long flat-muscled flanks. Sweat showed like oil against the smooth, pale-brown skin and small blurs of dirt lay on his shoulders; he had a wide chest for so small-waisted a man. She saw all this, careful to note it; her eyes held a screened darkness, her expression was steady and solemn. He said again, "Thanks," and took a quick look at the overhead sun, and sat down on the dirt pile to eat. He had big knuckles on his hands, and long fingers; he was slow moving, almost as slow moving as Henry Zimmer — but it was a different slowness.

She said: "You never farmed much, did you?"

"No," he said, "cows are my line."

"What's a cowpuncher doing on a homestead?"

"Well," he said, "I don't know." He sat a moment, thinking of this in the way he thought of so many things, closely and narrow-eyed, worrying it around his head. "Maybe it's because a man's got to put down some roots finally. Nothing for a fellow on the trail. Just a bunch of campfires. One day here, one day someplace else."

"I guess you've seen a lot of country. That must be nice. What's it like?"

"Just country," he said. "It ain't ever any different on the other side of the hill."

"Maybe," she said, "it will be different here."

He shrugged his shoulders. "I don't know. Maybe."

It was hard to know what he thought or what he felt when he used that tone. She knew her father and Henry Zimmer — and now even Cam Skelton. They were plain to her eyes; but this man was a stranger; he was not simple to read. Lisbeth reined her pony on to the new homestead shanty, softly sighing to herself, and got down. This house sat against the raw earth. There was no porch; only a single step leading into two small front rooms and a rear kitchen. The

171

smell of wood was clean and strong and resinous; there was nothing here at all, only bare, square walls and two windows and two doors; but she stood in the center of the place, thinking — this would be the bedroom. She would bring the rug for the floor, and the green-dotted curtains. She stood still, trying to reach into his mind and discover why he had built three rooms to the house when most men putting up the first homestead shack only built two.

She moved through the house to the back door. Framed in it, with her white strong arms stretched against the sides of the door and her upper body high and rounded and firm, she watched Law dump the dirt bucket and climb into the well again. He didn't look at her but she knew that he felt her presence, that he knew how close she was to him; he had just eaten and now without delay he was working, as though there was a restlessness he had to wear off. The well was close to the house and she saw that he had placed it so that another room and a porch would enclose it. There wasn't a tree for miles and no shade — nothing but the sage marching out of the flats to the very edges of this place; but she saw the square of poplars around this yard and the garden beyond the well, and the fruit trees. It would not be so long;

it would be nice to watch them grow. One thing, though. There would have to be a fence along the edge of the Silver Bow's canyon, to keep the babies from falling into it. Law climbed from the well again, hauling up the bucket. The muscles of his back were long and tight against the brown skin; when he bent over they disappeared and the dotted line of his spine showed white and broad. She said, "So-long," and didn't hear him answer; she rode on home across the canyon and fell to making bread in the warm drowse of the long afternoon, her hands patting the loaves into shape deftly, her thoughts running away from her hands.

At four she saw him riding back on the south rim of the canyon, long before he usually quit work; and stepping out to the rim she watched him stop in the bottom willows. Presently his body was a white and distant blur against the water as he took his swim; later, he rode across the yard. His head was still damp, black and glittering; and his expression was sharp. He said, "I won't be here for supper," and sent his pony townward, sitting in the saddle with that perfect looseness no homesteader could ever match.

She watched him until he was vague in the dust and the low slanting sunlight, and would have watched longer; but it was time to make supper. At six Henry Zimmer came out of the canyon, a loose lump on the faithful plowhorse, and her father walked back from the barn and the children suddenly ran in from all quarters of the prairie. She was silent in the supper table's robust racket, close-caught by her thoughts; she was remembering the little things about Bob Law, the way he watched the sky, the way he listened into the darkness, and half through the supper dishes she said, "I am going to town," and at once left the house to saddle her horse.

Dusk moved softly down; westward the band of light lying over the mountains began to narrow and lose clarity. At this hour, the silence was long and deep on the land and all the redolence of the prairie rose around her; the lights of Prairie City began to sparkle ahead. In town she dropped off at Wickert's store.

"I want," she said, "a little bottle of perfume. Just a little bottle."

She paid a dollar for it and was shocked at her extravagance. Night dropped suddenly and in the doorway of Wickert's she watched dust boil in the yellow out-thrown beams of the store lights; shadows made dark banks at wall and alley mouth. Here she stood when Bob Law came from Mike

Danahue's saloon farther along the street. The glow of the saloon caught him, his whip-shaped frame, his wide-spread legs and his head bowed beneath the flare of the broad cowpuncher's hat. He had been drinking. She saw that at once from the way he braced himself by the door. He turned from the door and went along the street, reaching out to steady himself by the saloon wall. At the far corner of the saloon, where the stairway ran up to the second floor, he stopped and turned toward the stairs. He didn't move; he just watched them.

Lisbeth got on her horse and went out of town. She wanted to look back to see if he had gone up the stairs, but she kept her eyes to the front. She knew him better now, a little better. Restlessness had driven him into town, to drink; loneliness turned him to the stairs. She thought about that all the way home. Henry Zimmer sat in his corner chair, square and speechless and making sharp little sounds with his lips as he sucked on his pipe; her father had the weekly paper spread under the table lamp's yellow cone, reading with a faint motion of his mouth. Lisbeth went on to her own room closing the door, so that none of them would see the perfume.

Even with the stopper in the bottle a

175

strong fragrance came out. She stood in the room's center, watching light turn tawny as it struck the bottle. She had never owned perfume and it was a little like sin to have it now. But she was thinking of the differences in men. A woman might give herself to Henry Zimmer, and get him; she might hint the same thing to Cam Skelton, and that would be enough. But not with Bob Law. The things he wanted were mysterious in the way they came to him — like the sound of the wind in the sage, like the sight of a mist cloud breaking on the saw-tooth summits of the hills; like, maybe, the scent of perfume on a woman's dress.

She opened the bottle and drew the wet cork once across the breastline of her waist and stood silent a moment, a lightness like a smile on her lips. This was to remind him that the faraway things he wanted were not as far as he thought; then she put the perfume in the drawer of her bureau and crossed back to the yard.

Half an hour later she saw him ride in and unsaddle his pony. He wasn't drunk now; he was slow and certain in the way he laid his shoulders against the corral to make up a cigarette. Matchlight exploded against his face; it was sharp and still restless. He didn't move, he didn't look at her — though she knew he was aware of her; always she knew that, and it was in her mind to cross to him when she heard the quick in-drive of two or three ponies from the dark.

They came rapidly into the yard, three of them, and stopped a little distance from Bob Law who turned away from the corral to face them. One of these men said in a cold, steady way:

"Listen, mister. The time ain't come when a granger can walk into my place, pick a free fight and bust my poker tables all to hell. There's the little matter of a back bar mirror smashed likewise. Maybe you took me for a sucker. Well, sir, I've handled some tough lads in my time and I propose —"

He was a heavy man and he left the saddle and walked on, his boots squealing in the yard's dust carpet. Her father came out of the door and Henry Zimmer came out and her father yelled: "Who's talkin' like that?" But nobody else said anything. The big man made the last few feet on the run, grunting as he struck out with his arms. Lisbeth saw Bob Law's cigarette go to the ground in a shower of fine sparks, she saw Law wheel backward against the corral bars and come forward again. These two were close and they were fighting, the sound of their fists and the sound of their breathing very plain in the night. The big man knocked Bob Law into the corral again; he kept going forward, heavy and determined, meaning to beat Law down. Lisbeth saw Law give ground and stop; he was swift as he moved, he made a circle around the big man and the big man's head began to snap back when Bob Law hit him; the big man said nothing at all but he pushed forward, trying to bring his knees into Bob Law's crotch. His head kept coming up and after that he hit nothing, for Bob Law's long arms, outreaching him, caught him in the belly and in the temples and on the chin; and then the big man went down.

But one of the others, still mounted, suddenly said: "Just hang tight there, mister," and looking over that way, Lisbeth saw a gun pointed at Law. There was a chopping block half across the yard, with an ax sunk into it. Lisbeth ran over and seized the ax; she put it over her head and fled across the yard toward the man with the gun who suddenly said: "Here — get that damned girl — !" But his horse shied away from the downswinging ax and from the corner of her eyes she saw Bob Law duck into his tent and come out again.

"All right," he said, "all right."

He was laughing, or so it sounded to Lisbeth. He had gotten his revolver and held it on the mounted men; it wasn't laughter really, she saw. He was only smiling, and he was pleased with the fight, he wanted to fight. A small streak of blood showed on his chin. He said:

"I guess I've torn up a few saloons in my time, friend. The trail is full of joints like yours. I think you're a tinhorn. Let's just see. I'll count five."

The big man pushed himself off the ground. He said, "Wait a minute. How the hell was I to know you're a cowhand? I thought you was a nester."

Sam Hurd yelled, "What's the difference?"

The big man said: "If you'd been raised in cattle country you'd know. The boys have their habits. Just a little fun at the end of a dreary day. No offense, friend."

Ax in hand, Lisbeth watched these three ride away. Henry Zimmer hadn't moved from the house doorway. Sam Hurd was swearing, "By God, whut you do, Bob?" But Bob Law turned back into the tent.

Lisbeth dropped the ax, suddenly following Law. There wasn't any light in the tent, but the house lamps touched the canvas wall and by this faded glow she saw him. He sat in a chair, slumped over with his hands on his face, and when he looked at her she saw only the weariness of his face. She dropped to her knees and her voice was quick. "I would have chopped his arm off. I would."

She was close to him, close enough for him to catch the odor of the perfume, and she knew he caught it. She always knew when he was aware of her; and he had always been aware of her, never openly showing it. It was something he seemed to fight against. He sat there, his long arms idle, not speaking but looking at her with that same hard set on his cheeks. She knelt back and stood up. Sam Hurd yelled from the yard, "Lisbeth, what you doing there?"

She said: "It just got weary for you, working alone. So you got drunk. Then you went to the stairway that goes above the saloon —"

He said quickly, "I didn't go up."

"Would it have been a help — if you had?"

"I didn't go up," he said again.

"So for you it wouldn't have been a help."

The perfume was a faint incense in the tent's warmth. When he rose from the chair he was a head taller; he looked down, something changing his look. He said: "I've been too close to you. Not good for a man —"

"Being lonely is like that," she said. "I know what you like to eat. I know what you like to hear. I guess I've paid attention to that. I was raised a farm girl. I know what's to be done. You made three rooms. What's the extra room for, Bob? What woman?"

He said slowly, "Is that all there's to it? Nothing else, Lisbeth?"

She said, "A house — with a man and wife in the same bed. It is something. There is a fire in the stove; it is warm when the wind blows, and you are not alone. That is something, too. But not all. The rest —"

She was smiling when she raised her arms. It was the perfume, she thought — the faint call of it, the mystery of the promise of it — which brought him forward. Lisbeth raised her head so that he might not be mistaken about her; and suddenly was within his tight arms, feeling his kiss. This was it, though it had no name. Being very full, and feeling that everything was right. A corner of her mind thought: We will move in when the well is dug. I will bring the extra dishes. He will never have to worry about the house, ever, because I will take care of it. But the feeling grew stronger and fuller, completely crowding her body. She would never regret the perfume. "Because —" And she bent back a little to say in a faint, shy voice: "The rest, the rest is love. That is it." This was what a good marriage meant.

Tavern at Powell's Ferry

The coach rolled southward from the river into the flat valley's haze with late September's dry dust smoking up from its wheels; and as it departed Joab Powell had once more the vaguely discomforting sense of being left behind, of missing passage to the unknown place which was his rightful destination.

It was not a new feeling, but it made him impatient to be troubled so late in life by the urges which belonged to a young man. He turned the ferry across a river so low and quiet upon its bed that the old gray horse, plodding the treadmill, made no work of it. The mountains bordering the valley sank away in first twilight, the surface of the river began to exhale a thin crystal fog, and the smell of the earth was sharp and heavy with the year's decay. One day a hard rain would slant out of the southwest, announcing winter.

He tied the ferry and let the horse into its pasture, moving along a path bordered by wild rose brambles whose seed pods hung fat and red. He studied the framework of the new gristmill as he passed toward the house, calculating the work done upon it this day; and he observed that young John Sharpp, employed as carpenter, now stood on the porch of the house talking to Elizabeth. Elizabeth laughed in her bright, half mocking manner and her hand touched John Sharpp and for a moment the man caught her arm and the two were playfully struggling. Then John Sharpp heard his step on the path and stepped away from Elizabeth with an embarrassed smile.

"She'll tease the wits out of you, John," said Joab Powell and passed into the house. But he was thinking to himself: "It is past time for her to be married."

He walked through the house to the kitchen, past his other daughter Anna who worked quiet and swift with the supper; he washed himself at the back porch well, put on his slippers, and moved back to the big room's table, upon which the oil lamps now were pleasantly shining. He sat down and waited for his daughters and for John Sharpp; when they were seated he bowed his face with its rusty-iron beard, said grace, and began his meal. Far away he thought he heard travelers on the road.

Sharpp said: "I have got the big timbers all hewed for the raceway."

"I'll help you set them in Monday," said Powell. The young man had a good, square face which looked honestly upon the world; he was steady, he was made for the long slow pull, he would season with the years as a good hardwood stick seasons, and he would never lie awake in bed asking questions which had no answers.

What did Elizabeth want with him — this daughter whose discontent came out of her like a heat to disturb everything about her? She was too pretty, she hated too quickly, she wanted things not to be had in this out-of-way spot whose high point was the daily passing of a stage. She was, Powell thought with a father's moment of stark realism, ripe and over-ready. He looked down the table and saw Anna looking on at Elizabeth and John Sharpp with her deep gravity.

A wagon came along with its racket and someone said, "This is Powell's," and voices began to rise in the yard. Anna left the table at once, moving toward the kitchen. Rising to meet his guests, Joab Powell noticed sudden interest brighten Elizabeth's face as she touched her hair and ran a finger along her eyebrows in expectation of new eyes to look upon her.

The travelers entered with the subdued bustle of weary people, a man and woman past middle age, a boy and girl in brash adolescence, a young woman with an attractive, pouting face, and a pair of men. One was thin and very darkly colored and possessing a pair of brows black as ink; the other, a blond gentleman with an extraordinarily regular profile, had a face which, seen face-on, showed some evidence of dissipation.

The elderly man said: "Thank God tomorrow is a day of rest. These Oregon roads are without question some kind of an approach to Inferno. We require accommodations until Monday morning. Can you put us up and, as a practical matter, what are your rates?"

Joab Powell said: "Two dollars the night and fifty cents the meal."

"Acceptable," said the older one. "You are looking upon Edward Ord Mainring's Theatrical Troupe, now on tour, presently bound to play the Jacksonville mines. Mrs. Mainring, if you please. Our young star, Miss Strange. My daughter Jo and my son Tarleton. My leading man, James Hawtree" — this was the one with the striking profile — "and Mr. Victor Porrocks, whose darker cast lends flavor to our villains."

The young man thus identified displayed a gentle smile while Mr. Hawtree cast a frankly speculative glance upon Elizabeth, who returned the glance with equal speculation, Miss Strange observed this exchange of interest and paid Elizabeth the courtesy of a moment's cold interest. Young Tarleton Mainring peevishly said, "I'm awful hungry."

"Elizabeth," said Joab Powell, "show these people their rooms."

Elizabeth moved to the stairs and ascended with a composed and excellent carriage; the members of the troupe, each with luggage, trudged after her and made some racket in the upper hall as they found their quarters. Joab Powell stepped from the house to direct the party's wagoner to the barn, and Anna quietly returned from the kitchen to set new places at the table. She looked at John Sharpp who sat alone before his unfinished meal; she caught his glance and smiled at him.

"Acting people?" he said. "Here?"

"This is a tavern, John." She circled the table, and when she got behind him she paused a moment, looking down on his head with a grave stillness on her face; then she moved back to the kitchen.

The party came down the stairs to their supper, cheerfully and with considerable noise. Joab Powell returned from the night;

he took his place again at the head of the table and sat over his coffee. They were a hungry lot, he observed; they were an odd assortment out of the kind of world he had almost forgotten. Mainring and Mainring's wife were pleasantly comfortable people; their children were brash, as their life had no doubt taught them to be. The fellow who was the villain seemed, in these surroundings, to be a mild and inconspicuous fellow; but Mr. Hawtree was of another breed. He saw Hawtree's eyes now and then lift and strike Elizabeth who, returned from upstairs, now stood in the background of the room with that quietness upon her which Joab Powell knew so well; there would be excitement playing beneath it and her discontent would be driving her toward a greater fury at her life. She stared at Hawtree steadily and Hawtree's expression revealed his rising instincts. John Sharpp saw none of this; he finished his meal in silence and rose and left the room. But Miss Strange — there was a girl with her own kind of knowledge, Joab Powell thought — saw it all and gave Hawtree her cutting glance.

Powell said: "If you're going to the mines, you'll only get that wagon as far as Canyonville. The road's nothing but a trail beyond. You'll need horses there."

Mainring leaned back from his plate, flushed and comforted; he was expansive, he was philosophical. "We shall not think of that until we reach Canyonville. In this profession, Mr. Powell, you do not worry about tomorrow too much. There are always contingencies, disasters and emergencies to be surmounted. Fire, flood, famine and mob. In forty years of trouping Mrs. Mainring and I have seen the ugly faces of them all. Here we are, lacking a player for the part of the plantation belle. Where shall we get her? I do not know. But it is three days to Jacksonville. We shall have her when we get there."

"Uncertainty would not please me," said Joab Powell.

"Uncertainty," said Mainring, "is youth. Have you forgotten how, as a boy, you counted on tomorrow's excitement and venture?"

Well, thought Joab Powell, the man did for a fact appear young. He had no particular lines on his face, his eyes were bright and he was at the present moment wholly happy, or seemed so. Elizabeth, he noticed, now moved slowly across the floor and stepped from the house. Suddenly Hawtree emptied his coffee cup and rose and walked after her.

Mainring said: "Bed will be a comfort

after these roads," and left the table. One by one the party moved up the stairs while Joab stood by the fireplace and watched Anna quietly come and go with her chores. Outside he heard Elizabeth's voice, sometimes slow, sometimes light, sometimes intemperately strong. Hawtree's tone was a sympathetic murmur. Joab pried a better flame from the fireplace logs, looked for his glasses and sat down in a rocking chair; he took up his pipe, filled and lighted it, and reached for his paper, which was from Portland. The crickets were full-voiced in the broad night and the air coming through the front door had its chill. For a moment his mind went idly around the circle of things to be done before winter came.

Hawtree moved into the house with an aggressive stride, his face square and flushed, and went stamping up the stairs. Hidden behind his paper, Joab Powell heard Elizabeth later enter the room. He had no wish to look at her at the moment. He said: "Help your sister," and listened to her steps go laggard toward the kitchen.

Half reading, he heard the house settle down. The murmuring above stairs slowly died away, and bodies turned upon their beds, and now and then a door closed. John Sharpp climbed the stairs, a young man solemnly displeased with the sudden turn of affairs, and Elizabeth came from the kitchen and for a moment paused. When Joab Powell lowered his paper he saw the bright burning of her eyes, the thoughts half-shaped upon her face. She was a stranger to him tonight, as she had been on so many other occasions; she was his flesh and his blood, but her spirit — whose was that? He wanted to speak to her and he saw that she wanted to speak to him, yet neither of them had a way of bridging the difference between.

He said: "Sharpp's a good young man. Don't use him hard, unless you mean to have him."

She laughed at him with her eyes, a hot, sharp and unamused laugh; then she climbed the stairs. In a little while Anna, having done the last of her chores, quietly followed. Joab said: "Good night, Anna." Her voice came back in its neverchanging way; it carried the melody that was in her and never left her.

"Good night."

He let the paper lie and be refilled his pipe, deeply breathing the smoke and finding relish in it. He was a stout, aging man, made benevolent in appearance by his beard and the tall dome of his forehead; it was a benevolence sharpened by a realism which forever colored his judgments. He thought: "John should be Anna's man. It would work better that way." He thought about Elizabeth and found no answer for her. He thought of the show troupe which was so gay and glamorous to Elizabeth's eyes but which was simply a group of tired people forever on the move to earn a threadbare livelihood, all their cheap trinkets contained in a few battered trunks. He knocked out his pipe and went slowly to his room. There was still a light in Elizabeth's room as he passed by.

The fall fog lay silver-thick over the river by morning and dew glistened on the earth until noon. Church was ten miles distant and therefore not always to be attended, but Joab Powell made grace at breakfast longer than usual, and had a special prayer at the midday meal. Thereafter, in a warm, half-clouded afternoon he did his chores and tended ferry. The north-bound stage crossed at two o'clock; the south-bound at four. During the day he saw Hawtree and Elizabeth walking together along the dusty road, and he saw John Sharpp sulking alone in his good clothes by the river. Mainring's youngsters, discovering the gristmill, climbed to the rafter peaks until they were tired; and borrowed a skiff and vanished beyond the willows. Near five o'clock Mainring walked to the ferry where Joab Powell idly worked, and sat himself on the treadmill. He was, Powell saw, not wholly at ease; and it occurred to Powell to wonder if the man were about to suggest a compromise on the lodging bill.

"I believe last night," said Mainring, "I mentioned we had lost one of our cast. She was a refined young lady with some talent who suddenly discovered domestic virtue in Portland and left us."

"Heard you mention it," said Powell.

"So did your daughter Elizabeth," said Mainring.

"My daughter Elizabeth," said Powell, "does considerable idle dreaming."

"It is a habit," said Mainring, "we all have. It is the way we all live. Make-believe."

"I don't," said Joab Powell.

"My friend," said Mainring, "have you never wished your ferry would carry you farther than that other bank of the river?"

"I know what's beyond the other bank," said Powell.

"Your daughter, being young, does not."

Powell said: "She's been talking to you. Asked you if maybe she had ability to act.

192

She's been acting ever since you set foot in the tavern."

"So she has," said Mainring. "Very indifferent acting, too."

Powell drove two nails deep with his hammer and straightened. He watched Mainring's children drift down the river in the rowboat, and he watched the afternoon's haze close upon the Cascades. He turned to Mainring. "I suppose she wants to go with you."

"Your daughter," said Mainring, careful and quiet, "is not happy here. I saw it at once."

"It is nothing a marriage won't cure."

Mainring said, "Have you got some tobacco?" He filled his pipe from Powell's pouch. He lighted the pipe and set it to burning with long, steady draws. "We put up for noon yesterday at a place. Man and wife. The wife was odd."

"Purdy's wife," said Powell, "is crazy."

"Her face bothered me a great deal after we left," said Mainring. "It was a haunted face. She watched us go. You could see she wanted to be with us. She wanted to be with anybody who was going away from that place. One day she'll sink an ax into Purdy's head when he isn't looking and she'll start walking. Where to? Any place away from where she is. Marriage didn't cure what was in her mind. Some people have to run. Nothing else will do."

Powell said: "Cheap and shoddy."

"You're no doubt thinking of Hawtree," said Mainring. "Have you got no Hawtrees in your neighborhood? Your daughter is in her own hands. Here or elsewhere she will make her own lot. But if you do not permit her to follow her desires, she will make a bad job of it. You will have another Purdy's wife. I have seen a great deal of this world. I have seen a lot of Purdy's wives."

"I have seen women who started out on a wild goose chase and ended common," said Powell. "There's more of them than Purdy's wives."

"Your daughter," said Mainring quite frankly, "could fill a place in my company. Nothing more. It will take me a great deal of time to teach her to open and shut a door on the stage. I can do that for her. If she has no ability, she will fail and she will come back. If she has ability she will go on and up. Either way, she will have had her run."

"No," said Powell, "she won't come back."

"Then," said Mainring, "she is the kind you could never hold in any event. If you try to hold her you will regret it and she will see to it that you regret it."

"Not to be thought of," said Powell.

Mainring rose and tapped out his pipe. "A man," he said thoughtfully, "has a duty to his children. Sometimes the duty is to let go, not to hold. The world is vile and she will be exposed to it. The world is great, and she is looking for greatness. How are you to know what will become of her? You will not know. But when any human soul cries out for release, vile or great, you cannot stop that soul from venturing. To your daughter, desperate for something she cannot find here, even the vile is better than nothing at all."

He moved up the trail to the house; and suddenly he turned about and said a last thing with some sharpness. "Look into your own heart, my friend," and went on.

The sun was somewhere low behind September's haze. There was a wind, slight and cool, out of the southeast; in another day or so, Joab Powell thought, the wind would swing and the hard, intemperate rain would come to freshen the earth. A wagon moved out of the north and onto the ferry and as he was about to cast off he saw Elizabeth move swiftly down from the house. She came aboard and rode in silence across the water; and she waited afterward until the wagon had gone on. Then she faced her father and he saw the gathering storm on her face, the intensity almost like pain, the wanting so crowded within her that it made shadows in her eyes. It came out of her — all this — in one awkward, swift phrase: "I've got to go with them."

The old gray horse plodded the treadmill and the ferry made its semicircular path on the water. Joab stood grave at the bow, meeting her eyes.

"Daughter," he said, "you have made a picture for yourself. You're seeing yourself as a great actress, people throwing flowers up to the stage, people pointing you out in restaurants where you eat. You're seeing strange towns through the world, and kings and queens sitting in opera boxes while you play. That's what you're seeing. When you were ten you saw the same things, standing in the hay loft, swinging your arms and talking to yourself."

"Why not?" she said. "Why not?"

"You think this shabby little troupe will do it for you? Playing in cheap mining camps, riding wet through the rain, living in rooming houses? Wearing your clothes after they've turned color, being with men like Hawtree?"

She said in the most calculating of ways:

"I know about Hawtree. I can take care of myself. I am harder than he is. How do you suppose people start? They've got to start small. I don't mind. But I've got to go with them. I can't stay here any more. You're old. You're happy. You don't see what I see. Why don't you let me go? Do you know what I'll do if you keep me here? I'll marry Sharpp. I'll make him miserable — I'll make Anna miserable because she wants him. Then I'll run away. Or I'll take the first well-dressed man who comes through here and I'll go with him. I have got to go!"

He had no answer for her; he was ashamed of what she had said and did not meet her eyes. He stooped, a little awkwardly, and tied the ferry to the shore; he let the gray horse into its pasture, watching Elizabeth go up the pathway, half running. He reached for his pipe and he filled it, and held it unlighted in his mouth. Darkness had begun to sweep down, drowning the hills and covering the valley's far run, swinging on forward with its shadows until the world was reduced to this small settlement beside the river. "Why," he thought, "it's late." Then he realized the darkness was the darkness of rain clouds moving slowly up. He walked toward the house and as he walked he began to think of his wife, long dead. He said to himself: "Annie, what's in that girl? What am I to do?"

He said grace over a full supper table and he ate in mild, steady detachment while talk boiled and bubbled around him. Elizabeth moved like an alien shadow about the room, darkly withdrawn from him; somehow in the space of an hour or so she had cut herself from this family and was no longer a part of it. He felt the hatred in her — the wild and passionate despair. It touched him like a disturbed air. John Sharpp, unfavorably silent, sat through the meal as a man perplexed by things he felt but could not understand, and soon withdrew from the house; and presently one by one the troupe climbed the stairs to bed. Joab Powell went out to do the night's chores and came back later through the kitchen to find John Sharpp in the kitchen with Anna, drying dishes. Elizabeth had gone up to her room. Her cruel mood had reached out to Sharpp, simple a man as he was, and had made him feel no longer near her; and now Sharpp returned to someone he could understand.

Joab Powell freshened the fire on the hearth and removed his shoes and sat once more in the rocker, comforted by all the sounds of this house. He lay back, feeling oldness come to him and the loneliness that always arrived with it. Elizabeth was on his mind and the puzzle of her temper grew greater to him. Where had she gotten that rebellion, that wild will, that hatred of old and familiar things?

John Sharpp presently trod upstairs in silence and later, with night's work done, Anna came into the room. She paused before Joab Powell, smiling down at him, and he saw a momentary happiness on her face. It was the little things she loved, the old ways, the comfortable and familiar habits of life. Yet, watching her, he saw the smile fade and her inner contentment go away. Her face mirrored the nearest expression of anger he had ever noticed there.

"Let her go, father. Let her leave!"

"Why daughter," he said, and was truly shocked. "Do you understand what might happen to her?"

"Do you know," she answered, as harsh and as sure as Elizabeth could be, "what is happening now while she stays? Don't hold her. She's entitled to be happy if she can. I'm entitled to be happy as well, am I not?"

She said no more. She bent forward and quietly kissed him and took the stairs; but Joab Powell thought with astonishment: "They are strangers side by side. They are not sisters."

The question came again to him, insistently demanding answer; from what source had come Elizabeth's discontent with the world as it was? He sat quite still in the room's silence, turning his thoughts upon himself. He was a solid man, wasn't he? He had found this place upon the earth, he had built his house and accumulated his goods and he was satisfied. Long ago as a boy he had possessed a boy's longings and a boy's impatience but never had he eaten out his heart over things that couldn't be. Yet now he remembered how he watched the stage each day disappear to the southward, and he recalled the strange and unknown currents which stirred in him as he saw it go.

The thought made him move slightly on the rocker; and then he got to thinking of his wife and he saw so clearly the outline of her placid face before him. She had been a fine woman, she had been beside him, without complaint, all the way along the years. Suddenly he sat forward in his chair, bringing to his mind something he had never cared to think much about. There had been a young man, long ago, in the Illinois town from which he and his wife had both come. Annie had liked that careless, devil-taken scoundrel whose name was Burge Simms — and Burge Simms had gone away to be a river pilot on the Mississippi. Maybe Burge had been the man Annie had wanted. He never had known about that, but often he had wondered about her thoughts when she sat so still by the evening fire, when she stood at the doorway and looked out upon the land. She had died smiling at him but, and he sat forward again with a stinging feeling on his face, she had also died with her innermost feelings still a mystery to him. He had wanted a quiet and solid woman; she had given him that, keeping the rest to herself.

Now a feeling came hard upon him, new to his practical mind, unsettling to his need of steadiness. Here his daughter Anna had stood a moment ago, revealing a passionate feeling he had not known she possessed; and upstairs all these various people slept, the saturnine Porrocks who played the part of a villain and yet was a gentleman, and Hawtree who was a hero on the stage and a shoddy character otherwise, and John Sharpp, so plain and steady a man. All these people lay on their beds now, all known to him in a way by their speech and the things which were upon their faces; but carrying dreams he couldn't know.

He laid a hand heavy upon the arm of the rocking chair and he said, aloud, but quiet:

"Why, nobody actually knows anybody else."

Rising, he followed the ritual of his life. He tested the door lock and screened the fire; he laid his pipe in its bowl and took up the lamp and slowly ascended the stairs. When he came to the door of Elizabeth's room he knocked, and heard her slow, sullen voice bid him in. She stood dressed in the middle of the room, and he saw that she had been walking restlessly around with her thoughts. Her eyes, turned to him, were alien.

"Elizabeth," he said, "you have got your own life to live. Go ahead and live it as you please." He drew back and quickly closed the door; but even so, he saw the light break across her face. She was like a prisoner getting news of release, he thought sadly.

It had rained during the night and had ceased. Now the quenched earth sent its raw fine smell into the morning, and a thick mist silvered the air so thickly that the cottonwoods of the far shore were vaguest shadows. The troupe's wagon stood by with the baggage loaded and the driver in his seat; the troupe came out, freshly rested, and eager to be going. Mainring paid his cheerful compliments to Joab Powell and the gentle villain shook Powell's hand. "I would not mind," he said, "trading places with you. It is a pleasant piece of earth here."

The wagon rolled aboard the ferry, the members of the troupe walking casually after. Joab Powell brought the old gray horse — its ancient muzzle a-sparkle with night's dew — out of the pasture to the treadmill and waited for the last passenger, Elizabeth.

She was at the house doorway, facing Anna; and he stood still, watching those two say their farewells, realizing that both girls were glad to have it this way. They kissed briefly and Elizabeth said one gay word in response to Anna's grave nod; then Elizabeth came down the pathway to where John Sharpp waited and she paused to look up at his grieving face. She laughed at him and said some soft thing, and kissed him lightly on the cheek and thereafter, like a delighted child, she ran down the path to the ferry. Joab cast off the line; the old horse, patiently plodding, started the ferry over the river.

The troupe was forward, near the team, deliberately giving Joab his privacy as Elizabeth stood by him. A fish jumped and made a widening circle on the water and the river made its washing sound on the mild rapids lower down. Joab stared away from his daughter.

"When I was young I wanted many things. I found out I couldn't have a lot of those things. It wasn't in me to have them. It may not be in you to have all that you want."

"Why," said Elizabeth, "I shall get what I want."

"You will try," said Joab Powell soberly, "and maybe that's the fun of it. But if you do not find what you want, come back. I'll be here." Then he added a grave afterthought. "Don't stay away too long. I'm not young."

"I'll come back to see you, of course," said Elizabeth in her light voice.

The ferry touched the south shore's mud bank and the team moved the wagon to land. Now the troupe members climbed aboard and the voices of all of them were gay with morning and with the excitement of being in motion. Joab turned to Elizabeth and saw the same excitement on her face, the fine flame in her eyes. She was trying to remember, he saw, that he was her father and that she was going away from him and should be sad. But even as she tried to remember that, she was still happy and could not show sorrow. She put her arms around him and kissed him fully, the first such kiss he could remember from her since she had been a child; and she stepped back, laughing, with her eyes moist. She turned and walked to the wagon and took her place on one of the seats. Mainring cried heartily out, "Tallyho," and the teamster's sharp shout put the horses forward.

Joab Powell watched wagon and people slowly grow obscure in the close-hanging mists. He saw them wave at him, he heard them pleasantly calling; they were like children off to a party, straining for new things and greater surprises beyond. Elizabeth raised her hand to blow him a kiss and Joab, memorizing her face with greatest care, lifted his own hand in return salute. Then the mists covered them and for a little while he heard their voices come back through the mists. Afterwards they were lost to him, sight and sound of them alike dying. He thought to himself: "I have got to remember what she looked like," and started the ferry away.

Half over the river he was alone in the mist, both shores dim. He loaded his pipe with a mechanical interest as he thought of her. He had asked her to come back and she had promised she would; but even then he knew she never would return. He had made the same promise to his own parents when he as a young man had left the Vermont farm, bound west to Illinois. Many times during the later years he had thought of his people, resolving to return to them for a visit; but he never had. Life was pretty much a parting of the young from the old; the young venturing away with their ambitions and the old settled fast to their comforts.

He tied the ferry and put the horse into its meadow and he stood facing the south shore, listening with the hope that he might hear one last sound return from the wagon. Anna and John came down the pathway; they stopped before him and he observed that they were sorry for him. They were good and simple people and they would do well together; they would fill this tavern with children and they would be content. It gave him comfort to think of it.

Anna said: "Don't worry, father. It is the first time she has really been happy."

Still thinking of Elizabeth, he was suddenly proud of her. She was breaking away to follow her wants, just as he had done. She was a piece of him venturing afar, doing those things he had wished to do and had never succeeded in doing. Each day now, as he watched the southbound stage roll away, he would scarcely need to feel that somehow he had missed his destination. Elizabeth took his place, and sought the destination.

Joab said: "We'll lay the timbers today,

John," and started up the pathway toward the gristmill. He thought to himself: *I shall have to remember how she looked, for I shall never see her again.*

Smoky in the West

He came up to the Reynolds ranch early that morning in a buggy drawn by two matched duns — not a big man but stocky and brisk, with bright hazel eyes set into a high-colored face. When Madge came out to the porch she saw the confident quality of his smile, as though even then he realized his power over people and circumstances, as though he had some clear intimation of his life to come. He said, in a voice that poorly controlled his impatience:

"If you choose, we can make it to my ranch by dark. I think six months is long enough. You can have George or you can have me and God knows I'll give you everything a man can make out of this land. There's something ahead for us. I want you. I can't talk it, but you ought to see it. That's why I'm here. It's how I feel. Only, six months is time enough to wait and I won't come again."

She said in a soft voice: "Now, Jim? Right now?"

He said, "Now," and long years afterwards she remembered the ring of that answer, its brusque force. For a little while she stood before him, feeling the violent compulsions of his restless will and the burning heat of his ambition. She knew she would go; yet even as she made her decision she had a voiceless regret for the things she was giving up and never would get from Jim Carran. Afterwards she turned into the house. Within a quarter hour, all her possessions in the rig, she was on the way to Fossil with him.

Fossil was five houses rising freshly from a virgin prairie. All the land swept away to the far blue of the Wildhorse Hills and the wind at this hour was sweet with the warmth and growth of first spring. They were married at Rice Stewart's little land office and then returned to the street and found George Berryman paused by the rig, his easy-going face showing a shock that for one moment was actually wild. This was the time when Jim Carran, having won, could be a little tolerant and a little contemptuous. He said, "You lose, George," and left the two of them there, going into the adjacent store. Coming out later, he saw that his wife had taken her seat in the buggy and had turned so that she might not face George Berryman; for he, gripping the buggy's side panel with both his great fists, was watching her in a manner Jim Carran never forgot. Jim Carran was a sharp man with his eyes and he saw something in the tightness of his new wife's lips that ran a prowling doubt through him and set up his instant temper. He got up in the buggy's seat and called: "You're a slow man, George — and that's no way to get things in this world," and ran the buggy out of town.

It was thirty-five miles to the Forks, a lovely haze spreading over the land and softening its shallow sweeping folds. Jim Carran, absorbing it all with his bright hazel glance, laughed silently as he drove, stirred by things he could not express. There was almost nothing said between them though once when he saw her look back to the dimming shape of Fossil he asked in his half-impatient way: "Forget something?"

"No," she said. "Nothing."

At dusk they came upon the hills and the house and sheds and corrals of his ranch, with his three hands waiting there for him. He said in his abrupt manner, "This is Mrs. Carran, boys." When they entered that long low house on the Forks Jim Carran was twenty-one and his wife nineteen; but in 1870 there was no twilight age between youth and maturity. Both of them had reached maturity five years before.

The Wildhorse Hills rose directly behind the yard of his ranch, thick with pine, and now and then in the depths of the night it was the call of the coyotes that woke him and made him remember he had a wife beside him. She lay wholly still, but from the strong and even run of her breathing he knew that she was not asleep. He could touch her and feel the passiveness of her body, he could sense its lack of resistance, its lack of answer for him. In the morning, sitting across the table from her, he understood that somewhere during the dark hours a part of her had slipped away from him. He had this acuteness, he had this power of knowing people; it was his strength always, it explained his whole life. Looking at her, so composed and so patient, with a pride that opened her prettiness, he saw the wall between them clearly and his passion for completeness of possession made him say:

"Then why didn't you marry George?"

For a moment he thought she would lie or show fear — things that he forever hated. This was his mistake, for she looked at him with a directness he could not misunderstand. "I didn't love him."

"Nor me."

"There are things in you I like. And I could not stay single. I am nineteen, which is time to be married. What you want done, I will do."

This was his wife, governed by a realism he had to admire even while his impatient will struck against the reserve she showed him. In a way Jim Carran's mind had always been old, furnished in the beginning with a wisdom that controlled the restless energies boiling through his compact body. People could be persuaded, or bought, or broken. Most people. But he saw something in his wife that held him quiet in his chair and, during those few quiet moments, laid the whole pattern of his relations with her. She would bend but never break; soft as she was, she had her own will — and there was something in her mind or in her heart he could not own or share. This he knew to be so, though he didn't know why, and never knew.

She said: "You want me to go back?"

"No," he said, and his laugh was quick and full. In a way it was touched by the irony of this situation. "I wanted a wife. I wanted you. You will never be sorry."

Two mornings later he rode out of the Forks, bound for Texas with his foreman, Bill Gilbert, and three others, leaving one man behind to keep the place. Fifteen hundred miles down the trail lay Texas and cheap beef.

This was the central fact of Jim Carran's life, this sense of time cheating a man out of his good years. It made him hate delay and uncertainty, it made him drive others as he drove himself, with an inward fury. All this land was fresh and free and full of fortune to the proper man. There were times on that wild southward ride when Bill Gilbert, waking fitfully from a dog-tired sleep, saw Jim Carran crouched over the dying fire, stone-still and brooding out his thoughts; there were times on that hard trip when he saw Jim Carran's impatience spill over in great sudden swings of his hands against the saddle, as though he tried to use his physical strength to push the horse faster. Deep in Texas they bought up a thousand head of gaunt, southern beef and turned it north for the fattening grasses of the Forks. At the Cimarron crossing they were jumped by a party of four trail cutters. Jim Carran said: "Gentlemen, what do you wish?" He knew what they wanted, but he waited to be sure and when they told him he only added, "All right," which was a signal. After they crossed the Cimarron, Bill Gilbert looked behind him and saw the buzzards wheeling over the trail cutters now dead on the sandy earth.

In '75 the land was like that and men were like that. Bill Gilbert knew something about Jim Carran then that made his voice softer; and later, near a little town up on the Niobrara, he learned more. Jim Carran had gone in to have a drink. Three hours later, Bill Gilbert went in to see what delayed his return and found Jim Carran sitting at a saloon table with his back to a rear wall, laughing at the marshal who stood in the door and was afraid to fire. The saloon was broken up and there were two women sitting with Jim Carran, both laughing and Jim Carran's hazel eyes were pale and bright with drink and with the little devils of a starved temper furiously alive.

So Jim Carran came back to the Forks with his thousand cattle and four cowhands ridden gaunt, though he himself remained untouched by the journey. The ruddy blood showed on his cheeks when he came before his wife, and his laughter was full and frank, rolling out the great vigor in him; and when he kissed her it was in his mind that the hardness of his feeling would reach through her gravity and melt the barrier between. But the passiveness held, and then they were two people face to face, with everything as it had been before. He had brought back a silver-mounted saddle, and a package.

"The saddle," he said, "is for the boy, when he comes. The package is for you."

It was the costume of a Mexican dancer, even to the castanets and high bone comb. He saw the oddness in her cheeks, almost like pleasure, and said: "I met her somewhere in Texas. She was a dark woman — and very pretty. But not like you, Madge."

Her expression changed and she said, "Thank you," and he never saw the costume again. The saddle he hung in the front room as a reminder of the son he expected; and at those rare times when he remained home Madge Carran used to see him come before it, his eyes held by the flash and glow of the silver trimmings. His compact shoulders had a way of lifting and his words had a swing to them, thrown outward by the gustiness of his will. "I intend to leave the boy something when I die."

But it was a girl and he was not there at the time. Talk of a railroad was in the wind and he had gone off to Omaha to use his influence. Threshing back to the Forks in the dead of winter, he found his wife in the care of a woman from Sixty-Mile ranch. There had been no doctor. He stood awhile in the bedroom, showing very little of his feelings. Madge said: "I'm sorry you are disappointed."

"Her name," he said, "will be Caroline, which was my mother's name," and left the bedroom. He paused in front of the silver saddle a considerable interval, rocking on his heels; and afterwards went outside.

The second girl, Louisa, was born one year later; the following year the boy came. It was the last of their children, and, as with the others, he was away from the ranch. He stood again in his wife's room, the ruddiness of his cheeks showing clearly the pride he felt, as though he had seen the long battle through, as though he had put his will to this and won again. He said: "I am pleased, as any man should be. You will never regret it. His name, of course, will be Jim."

She looked up at him with that old expression which, acute of mind as he was, he could never fathom. And said: "Jim George Carran. You won't mind that?"

"No," he said. "No."

But when he next drove into town he went straight to George Berryman's store. "George," he said in a way wickedly civil, "my son has your name for a middle handle. It may be I was mistaken about you in the beginning."

Berryman's big hands roved the counter

top, and stopped. He was a quiet man, an easy-going man. But he came out from behind the counter and his voice was new to Jim Carran then. "I do not like the way you treat her and I do not like your talk. You want any more?"

Jim Carran's hazel eyes brightened; they grew round and almost pleased. "No," he murmured, "no more talk," and sprang at George Berryman. The big man moved back, taking Carran's fists on his chest; and reached out and struck Carran down at a single blow. He stood there, his breathing a little deeper, watching Carran come up and come on again. The scuffle of their boots made low sounds in the store and the beat of Carran's fists laid flat echoes across the heat. George Berryman knocked him down again — and saw the little man come up, the expression of his face bad to see, and Berryman knew Jim Carran would kill him or be killed; and afterwards Berryman slugged all consciousness out of Jim Carran in a sudden cold hatred and stood back a long while waiting for Carran to come to life. He had broken Carran's nose and beaten his lips to soft crimson. But Carran said: "All right, George. All right" — and went out of the store.

These were the growing years. The railroad came through and Fossil's street crawled along the tracks, and loading pens appeared, and a man came in and set up a bank with Jim Carran's support. Settlers began to break the uniform sweep of the land with their windmills on Dutch Flats. Once a nester came into the Forks country and put up his shanty, which pleased Madge.

She said: "I'll be glad to have them as neighbors."

That night Jim Carran took Bill Gilbert and rode the five miles across country to the nester's shack. There was a moment when it might have been bad, for the nester stood up against his house with a lifted rifle — a slim Missourian with a wife and half a dozen kids. "The land," he said, "is plumb free."

There was that moment when it might have been bad. But Jim Carran kept hold of the man's eyes and finally he laughed and got out of his saddle, and went forward and knocked down the rifle. He said, "Pack up and move. This is cow country." Half an hour later he threw five twenty-dollar gold pieces into the nester's departing wagon — and touched a match to the shanty. It made a great orange bomb in the sky as he rode home with Bill Gilbert and was even visible from the Forks ranch. Madge Carran saw it and turned slowly away, not speaking. But two years later she made her answer. "Caroline will be ready for school next year and there are no neighbors here to make a school. We'll have to move to Fossil."

It was the day of the great, square stone town house for cattlemen and Jim Carran, riding up to wealth on his blocky beeves, built such a house on the outskirts of Fossil and planted a double row of poplars entirely around it. He bought a great iron stag in Omaha and set it in the front yard; and high on the windmill tower he had the brand of his outfit painted in white letters: Lazy JC. So, seven years from the day Madge Carran stepped into the house on the Forks, she stepped out of it — and never lived there again. Riding into Fossil that day, she looked back once at the outline of the ranch quarters at the base of the Wildhorse Hills, and remembered the calling of the coyotes on the black night of her arrival; and turned about, her shoulders held rigid.

He saw little of her, and little of his growing children; for these were his great years. The days of the saddle trip into Texas went away with the coming of steel, but each spring found him on the roundabout train journey, to Abilene or the deep Gulf country. Fall saw him riding the growing reaches of his own range; and winter was the time he built his political influence, in Washington, in the state capitol. For he was Jim Carran of the Forks now, a cattleman of the straight breed, and power fed on power and men could be bought or whipped or persuaded. Most men.

Yet there never was a time when the shape and quality of his wife didn't color his thoughts and lay against him a faint, insistent pressure. Of wonder. Of regret. Once, riding into Omaha, he casually met a woman, attracting her by that vitality and that willful personality which so inevitably compelled all people. At the station he said: "Perhaps I can be of some help to you, to your hotel," and watched the forming smile on her lips when she said, "Perhaps you can." And at times like those he judged women by the dignity of his wife's eyes — and found them all wanting.

Victory was an easy thing to him and his restlessness rose greater. Yet now and then the fire intermittently flickered out and left him gray-minded and oppressed by some vague shadows whose substance he could never touch and never define; and these were the times when Jim Carran broke away from wherever he was and ended up in some smoky, wicked trail dance hall along the cattle trail, his compact shoulders bunched over a table, his stubby hands gripping bottle and glass while mystery closed down and had its terrible way with him.

It was in '79 that the bank he had so carefully nourished shut its doors, the cashier missing; and somewhere during the day a homesteader, bearing a redoubled hatred of Jim Carran faced him on Fossil's street and put a bullet through his arm. Carran's replying shot killed the homesteader, but when George Berryman came running up, Jim Carran hadn't moved from his tracks. He said then, the blood dripping freely into the dust, "You're going to run that bank, George. You're the only man I have ever trusted. I'm personally responsible for every dime — and I will pay it."

These were the times that the sources of his power showed through. Afterwards, in the big stone town house he watched the alternate darkness and light give expression to his wife's eyes while the doctor worked on the torn arm. His son Jim-George stood beside his mother, eight years old and turned pale by what he saw.

It was that pallor which brought up something long dormant in Jim Carran, a resolution so far unkept. That summer he took Jim-George down to the Forks ranch, and rode through the Wildhorse Hills with him.

It was Jim-George's riding he kept watching, and Jim-George's character; for Jim Carran's sharp eyes had seen something he didn't like. But he kept his own counsel for four years, giving the boy credit he would never have given another man. Until, one day from his seat on the top bar of a corral he watched Jim-George leave a bucker in a long, low dive. Dust settled and silence came on. Jim-George got up, one shoulder lower than the other, his chalky cheeks tipped toward Jim Carran, and toward Bill Gilbert also watching.

"Hurt?"

"No," said Jim-George, and went back to the horse. Bill Gilbert helped him on; and the boy rode it through. But afterwards Jim Carran said:

"You're afraid of horses, Jim-George," and left the corral. He had no way of holding it back for he was a man who hated uncertainty and fear and all the small evasions of life. He saw the expression in his son's eyes as he turned from the corral, an expression terribly proud and mortally wounded — like that expression he had noticed so often in the eyes of his wife. He knew then he had pushed his son definitely away from him.

It was part of the price he paid for the heat of a will which wilted all that came before it; his victories came of that heat, and his defeats came of it, too, for his wife lay somewhere behind a reserve impenetrable to him, and now his son withdrew. The youngest girl, Louisa, grew up in the image of her mother, the same patience and the same far thoughts in her young eyes, and only in the oldest child, Caroline, did he see the reflection of himself — the mirrored laughter and impatience, the almost greedy love of life. Between them, from beginning to end, was a speechless closeness, an understanding he could never reach with others. Yet, in the long soft evenings of fall when he sat on the porch of the great stone house and heard her voice rise gaily among the voices of the boys in the yard, he sometimes sat quite still, held by a doubt and by a fear. He knew his own weaknesses: and saw them in Caroline.

So these years went, the streets of Fossil growing a little longer and the shade trees growing up to first maturity on soil that had been virgin in '70. Around this town lay the close-fenced homesteads of German settlers; and dusty roads began to lengthen away to other little towns and only in the far country about the Wildhorse Hills did cattlemen remain undisturbed. There was a time when the rustler grew great and when Jim Carran collected his own chosen men and scoured the Wildhorse pines and left those men hanging dead from the cottonwood branches along the isolated creek bottoms. There was a time when the sheepman moved his herds up from the Colorado parks — and retired again with his sheep lying in white, lifeless windrows at the base of the Porcupine cliffs. Jim Carran was in that, too. These were the hard years, the great and winey years when his life rolled up to its turbulent crest and when his signature was good on a check all the way from Texas to Wyoming. He was stockier than in the beginning and the ruddiness of his face had permanently deepened, leaving faint blood veins tracked against the skin.

Madge said: "Caroline is eighteen and a little wild. You should talk to her. And I wish you'd not let Jim-George ride so many horses. He has broken too many bones."

He had nothing he could say to his daughter when she came before him. For she was a formed, red-lipped woman and her eyes, as light as his own, knew all that he knew, leaving him helpless. It was in the spring of the year. She did something then she had never done before. She was laughing and she bent down and kissed him, but when she straightened he saw tears in her eyes. The week following she ran away from town with a transient man none of them knew. Once there was a letter from her with a St. Louis postmark. After that the long years closed down and they never heard of her again.

He knew as soon as she left that he had lost the only tie binding him to his family. And so it was a fear that made him take his son along on the next trip to Texas. Fear, and a desire to get nearer this son who, like Madge, stood so distant from him. Riding down the illimitable west, he kept remembering the look in Jim-George's eyes that day he had spoken of horses. It kept coming back to him, and impelled him to say: "Some men can ride, Jim-George, and some can't. It is no reflection on a man if he can't. But if he can't, all the trying in the world won't help. You're old enough now to know that. Better quit trying to ride the buckers." But from his son's deep silence he knew he had made no amends. The boy had a pride like his mother's pride — hidden far away in him, metal-hard.

There was that unease between them Jim Carran made his honest attempt to break. He knew of only one way, which was to show Jim-George the sort of a man he, Jim Carran, actually was. Truthfully and without those evasions which he so fundamentally hated. He was conscientious about it, retravelling the trail for his son's sake, introducing him to all the hale and earthy and large-handed men who were his own friends. "This," he would say, "is my son, Jim-George, who rides this way when I'm gone," and he would stand back to see how Jim-George caught on. There was a free-masonry on the trail. A man belonged or he didn't belong and presently he knew Jim-George didn't belong. It was a way of looking at life, a spirit that rode through trouble and misfortune, a laughter that drew men together, an appetite that reached vigorously and broadly and sometimes sinfully, into the depths of living. In a way Jim Carran's generation was a generation of lusty savages.

It was what Jim Carran felt, and wanted Jim-George to feel; and it was that great desire that impelled him, in a moment of terrible candor, to take Jim-George to one of those smoky and wicked road houses that he knew so well, so that Jim-George would know something of the secret turnings of a man's nature. Of women and drink, and some groping for a meaning to things, and some search for beauty, even within the four gray walls of a joint, with a pair of girls sitting at the table and a bottle of whisky standing half-empty there. But he saw Jim-George shrink and grow cold, and at that moment he recognized Madge's eyes looking directly at him.

The next day Jim-George started home with twenty car-loads of beef and Jim Carran took the rest of his trip alone. He was somewhere on the border a month later, when Madge's telegram caught up with him. Jim-George had been killed on a bucking horse.

He had been a week late for this boy's birth; he was a week late for his funeral. Standing alone — so thoroughly alone — in the soft prairie twilight, beside the freshly mounded earth, Jim Carran went down into the blackness that could come only to a self-sufficient man at last realizing what self-sufficiency had done to him. He remembered the way Jim-George had last looked at him across that wide gulf neither of them had ever been able to bridge; and he knew his few careless words, spoken so long ago, had killed Jim-George. The kid had tried to overcome his fear with bad horses, and in trying had died. It occurred to Jim Carran at this moment that Jim-George had, somewhere in his heart, wanted to be like his father.

There was a silence in the big stone house for Jim Carran, that terrible silence following the sound of voices and laughter and young people calling. Sitting in the living room with Madge and Louisa, who was another Madge in every gesture, Jim Carran found himself tight in his chair, waiting for Jim-George to speak, waiting for Caroline to come gaily through the front door. And then it was hard to let his muscles go slack and sit with the light shining in his eyes and watch Madge's fingers work through her knitting needles. Once he said:

"The blame is mine."

It was all he ever said, directly. Madge Carran's fingers came to a complete stop. She looked at him and in the long interval he saw, because his eyes had never lost their sharpness, that she was trying to find words that would ease it for him. Trying and failing. When she did speak it was to say something he never quite understood, such being the strange distance of her thoughts. "There are times, Jim, when I think I have misjudged you."

"Maybe we better go south for a trip this fall."

"Louisa is to be married then. Anyhow it is a little late for that."

It was a little late for a good many things. Riding out the summer along the old trails of the Wildhorse, he had certain spots on the hill heights from which he could see his range strike away in low undulations toward a misty horizon. All this belonged to him, the fruits of his restless years and his hard years. Yet he knew his time drew nearer its end, as with all the other great cattlemen. He was an island against which the waters of homestead settlement slowly rose and nothing held this range together but his own will. After him came the breakup. In Fossil now were the spindles of barb wire and the long piles of fence posts and the red painted plows awaiting that breakup.

So, then, what was his life for? This was the question that lay in Jim Carran's fertile mind as he rode his graze and saw his white-faced cows browsing, as he sat by night before the campfire of his round-up crew and watched the flames with the same furious energies having their way with him. This was as Bill Gilbert used to see him in the old trail days, and this was as he still remained, though times had changed and Bill Gilbert was gone. It was the thing he thought of on the long trips to the south, and in the murky confusion of the road houses on a trail almost vanished, and in the rooms of many a western hotel where he stopped to cement his business deals and brighten old time friendships.

There were, he saw, gray heads among those friends; and it reminded him suddenly that his own head was likewise graying, though this knowledge he kept pushing away. He was still an abrupt, stocky figure with the extreme ruddiness of cheek and the same high and explosive laugh; and in him still was the pent-up energy of a man searching for something to win. But the time for that was at an end. He had made his winnings.

For him there was no mellowness of age to absorb the shock of growing old; no dying out of the full fire of his will. In the beginning he had known his power, and knew it now in a way that made him brace the high desert wind and stiffen his shoulders and look into the distance with the desire to be again driving forward. Only, there was a difference. Once the distance had been empty; now there was no emptiness left for him to ride.

There was the time when he received notice of a pioneers' convention to be held at Ogallala. He read it and tore it up angrily, in front of George Berryman. "Pioneer, hell. I'm a young man and I don't go around croaking of the old days." But later that night he asked Madge in a slow, slow voice: "Has it been that long ago? What's happened to all that time?"

Coming out of the Wildhorse Hills one fall day in 1905, he stopped to open a gate of the Forks ranch and let his rifle slip awkwardly from his hands; and took a bullet into that arm which, years before, had been ripped by the crazed homesteader's shot.

The doctor in Fossil ordered him to bed, but he would not go until, on the third day, he felt the hurt climb slowly out of his arm into his shoulder. Then he knew the resistance of his youth was gone. On the fourth morning he called in George Berryman. "I want you to send two thousand dollars to Doña Anna Ramirez of Phoenix."

"Paying your bills?" asked George.

"I never dodged one."

"No," said George Berryman, gravely, "you never did, Jim."

This was a thing his mind dwelled on as the fever went up and his thoughts began to cross into that strange land of shadow. He had paid his bills, every one and it was a source of satisfaction. There were other people in the bedroom, their faces blurring. And a voice, kept saying: "I remember the time when Jim and me —."

Jim Carran said: "Jim-George come back from the Forks yet?"

"No, not yet."

"Tell him I want to see him. Why does Caroline stay out of the room so much?"

"They will come, Jim."

But he was thinking of something else. "Another time and another place and I might have made something of my life."

"Jim, what do you regret?"

It was a question that drew him back, out of a hot, bright land into a cool one. Lamplight glowed against evening's long dusk, and Madge stood over him. The tick of an alarm clock made an abnormally loud noise. He tried to lift his hand toward his wife, but though his will went into his muscles his arm never stirred; and he knew then he had come to the end of his time. She wasn't, he saw, crying and that didn't surprise him. She had never been a woman to show her feelings, or give way to the things most women did. It was a pride that held her up; it was a pride which even, in some of his smokiest hours, laid gentleness and a mystery on him. She was a fair woman, looking down with a faithfulness which supported him as he went out.

He said distinctly, "I am a wealthy man, but I have lost too much. That is what I regret. It occurs to me that in all these years I have never said that I loved you. I do. You are the one woman in the world I have ever loved, or respected."

Just before he died, and while he was aware of the outer world, she reached down and kissed him; and then he saw that there were tears in her eyes. Her fingers held his arm; they made a steady pressure, as though she were guiding him on his trip. It came to him then as his final thought that this gentle pressure had guided him all his days and had colored his world for him in strange ways. And so he died, as close to the meaning of his life as he ever got.

George Berryman came in at that moment and saw this little scene, with Madge Carran bent over the bed. He didn't speak till she had risen. Then he said:

"The man was great. He really was. None of his sins were small."

A Day in Town

They reached Two Dance around ten that morning and turned into the big lot between the courthouse and the Cattle King Hotel. Most of the homesteaders camped here when they came to town, for after a slow ride across the sage flats, underneath so hot and so yellow a sun, the shade of the huge locust trees was a comfort. Joe Blount unhitched and watered the horses and tied them to a pole. He was a long and loose and deliberate man who had worked with his hands too many years to waste motion, and if he dallied more than usual over his chores now it was because he dreaded the thing ahead of him.

His wife sat on the wagon's seat, holding the baby. She had a pin in her mouth and she was talking around it to young Tom: "Stay away from the horses on the street and don't you go near the railroad tracks. Keep hold of May's hand. She's too little to be alone, you remember. Be sure to come back by noon."

Young Tom was seven and getting pretty thin from growth. The trip to town had him excited. He kept nodding his sun-bleached head, he kept tugging at little May's hand, and then both of them ran headlong for the street and turned the corner of the Cattle King, shrilly whooping as they disappeared.

Blount looked up at his wife. She was a composed woman and not one to bother people with talk and sometimes it was hard for a man to know what was in her mind. But he knew what was there now, for all their problems were less than this one and they had gone over it pretty thoroughly the last two-three months. He moved his fingers up to the pocket of his shirt and dropped them immediately away, searching the smoky horizon with his glance. He didn't expect to see anything over there, but it was better than meeting her eyes at this moment. He said in his patiently low voice: "Think we could make it less than three hundred?"

The baby moved its arms, its warm-wet fingers aimlessly brushing Hester Blount's cheeks. She said: "I don't see how. We kept figuring — and it never gets smaller. You know best, Joe."

"No," he murmured, "it never gets any smaller. Well, three hundred. That's what I'll ask for." And yet, with the chore before him, he kept his place by the dropped wagon tongue. He put his hands in his pockets and drew a long breath and looked at the powdered earth below him with a sustained gravity, and was like this when Hester Blount spoke again. He noticed that she was pretty gentle with her words: "Why, now, Joe, you go on. It isn't like you were shiftless and hadn't tried. He knows you're a hard worker and he knows your word's good. You just go ahead."

"Guess we've both tried," he agreed. "And I guess he knows how it's been. We ain't alone." He went out toward the street, reminding himself of this. They weren't alone. All the people along Christmas Creek were burned out, so it wasn't as if he had failed because he didn't know how to farm. The thought comforted him a good deal; it restored a little of his pride. Crossing the street toward Dunmire's stable, he met Chess Roberts, with whom he had once punched cattle on the Hat outfit, and he stopped in great relief and palavered with Chess for a good ten minutes until, looking back, he saw his wife still seated on the wagon. That sight vaguely troubled him and he drawled to Chess, "Well, I'll see you later," and turned quite slowly toward the bank.

There was nothing in the bank's old-fashioned room to take a man's attention. Yet when he came into its hot, shaded silence Joe Blount removed his hat and felt ill at ease as he walked toward Lane McKercher. There was a pine desk and on the wall a railroad map showing the counties of the Territory in colors. Over at the other side of the room stood the cage where McKercher's son waited on the trade.

McKercher was big and bony and gray and his eyes could cut. They were that penetrating, as everybody agreed. "Been a long time since you came to town. Sit down and have a talk," and his glance saw more about Joe Blount than the homesteader himself could ever tell. "How's Christmas Creek?"

Blount settled in the chair. He said, "Why, just fine," and laid his hands over the hat in his lap. Weather had darkened him and work had thinned him and gravity remained like a stain on his checks. He was, McKercher recalled, about thirty years old, had once worked as a puncher on Hat and had married a girl from a small ranch over in the Yellows. Thirty wasn't so old, yet the country was having its way with Joe Blount. When he dropped his head the skin around his neck formed a loose crease and his mouth had that half-severe expression which comes from too much trouble. This was what McKercher saw. This and the blue army shirt, washed and mended until it was as thin as cotton, and the man's long hard hands lying so loose before him.

McKercher said, "A little dry over your way?"

"Oh," said Blount, "a little. Yeah, a little bit dry."

The banker sat back and waited, and the silence ran on a long while. Blount moved around in the chair and lifted his hand and reversed the hat on his lap. His eyes touched McKercher and passed quickly on to the ceiling. He stirred again, not comfortable. One hand reached up to the pocket of his shirt, dropping quickly back.

"Something on your mind, Joe?"

"Why," said Blount, "Hester and I have figured it out pretty close. It would take about three hundred dollars until next crop. Don't see how it could be less. There'd be seed and salt for stock and grub to put in and I guess some clothes for the kids. Seems like a lot but we can't seem to figure it any smaller."

"A loan?" said McKercher.

"Why, yes," said Blount, relieved that the explaining was over.

"Now, let's see. You've got another year to go before you get title to your place. So that's no security. How was your wheat?"

"Burnt out. No rain over there in April."

"How much stock?"

"Well, not much. Just two cows. I sold off last fall. The graze was pretty skinny." He looked at McKercher and said in the briefest way, "I got nothing to cover this loan. But I'm a pretty good worker."

McKercher turned his eyes toward the desk. There wasn't much to be seen behind the cropped gray whiskers of his face. According to the country this was why he wore them — so that a man could never tell what he figured. But his shoulders rose and dropped and he spoke regretfully: "There's no show for you on that ranch, Joe. Dry farming — it won't do. All you fellows are burned out. This country never was meant for it. It's cattle land and that's about all."

He let it go like that, and waited for the homesteader to come back with a better argument. Only, there was no argument. Joe Blount's lips changed a little and his hands flattened on the peak of his hat. He said in a slow, mild voice, "Well, I can see it your way all right," and got up. His hand strayed up to the shirt pocket again, and fell away — and McKercher, looking straight into the man's eyes, saw an expression there hard to define. The banker shook his head. Direct refusal was on his tongue and it wasn't like him to postpone it, which he did. "I'll think it over. Come back about two o'clock."

"Sure," said Blount, and turned across the room, his long frame swinging loosely, his knees springing as he walked, saving energy. After he had gone out of the place McKercher remembered the way the homesteader's hand had gone toward the shirt pocket. It was a gesture that remained in the banker's mind.

Blount stopped outside the bank. Hester, at this moment, was passing down toward the dry-goods store with the baby in her arms. He waited until she had gone into the store and then walked on toward the lower end of town, not wanting her to see him just then. He knew McKercher would turn him down at two o'clock. He had heard it pretty plainly in the banker's tone, and he was thinking of all the things he had meant to explain to McKercher. He was telling Mc-Kercher that one or two bad years shouldn't count against a man. That the land on Christmas Creek would grow the best winter wheat in the world. That you had to take the dry with the wet. But he knew he'd never say any of this. The talk wasn't in him, and never had been. Young Tom and little May were across the street, standing in front of

Swing's restaurant, seeing something that gripped their interest. Joe Blount looked at them from beneath the lowered brim of his hat; they were skinny with age and they needed some clothes. He went on by, coming against Chess Roberts near the saloon.

Chess said: "Well, we'll have a drink on this."

The smell of the saloon drifted out to Joe Blount, its odor of spilled whisky and tobacco smoke starting the saliva in his jaws, freshening a hunger. But Hester and the kids were on his mind and something told him it was unseemly, the way things were. He said: "Not right now, Chess. I got some chores to tend. What you doing?"

"You ain't heard? I'm riding for Hat again."

Blount said: "Kind of quiet over my way. Any jobs for a man on Hat?"

"Not now," said Chess. "We been layin' off summer help. A little bit tough this year, Joe. You havin' trouble on Christmas Creek?"

"Me? Not a bit, Chess. We get along. It's just that I like to keep workin'."

After Chess had gone, Joe Blount laid the point of his shoulder against the saloon wall and watched his two children walk hand in hand past the windows of the general store.

Young Tom pointed and swung his sister around; and both of them had their faces against a window, staring in. Blount pulled his eyes away. It took the kids to do things that scraped a man's pride pretty hard, that made him feel his failure. Under the saloon's broad awning lay shade, but sweat cracked through his forehead and he thought quickly of what he could do. Maybe Dunmire could use a man to break horses. Maybe he could get on hauling wood for the feed store. This was Saturday and the big ranch owners would be coming down the Two Dance grade pretty soon. Maybe there was a hole on one of those outfits. It was an hour until noon, and at noon he had to go back to Hester. He turned toward the feed store.

Hester Blount stood at the dry-goods counter of Vetten's store. Vetten came over, but she said, "I'm just trying to think." She laid the baby on the counter and watched it lift its feet straight in the air and aimlessly try to catch them with its hands; and she was thinking that the family needed a good many things. Underwear all around, and stockings and overalls. Little May had to have some material for a dress, and some ribbon. You couldn't let a girl grow up without a few pretty things, even out on Christmas Creek. It wasn't good for the girl.

Copper-toed shoes for young Tom, and a pair for his father; and lighter buttoned ones for May. None of these would be less than two dollars and a half, and it was a crime the way it mounted up. And plenty of flannel for the baby.

She had not thought of herself until she saw the dark gray bolt of silk lying at the end of the counter, and when she saw it something happened to her heart. It wasn't good to be so poor that the sight of a piece of silk made you feel this way. She turned from it, ashamed of her thoughts — as though she had been guilty of extravagance. Maybe if she were young again and still pretty, and wanting to catch a man's eyes, it might not be so silly to think of clothes. But she was no longer young or pretty and she had her man. She could take out her love of nice things on little May, who was going to be a very attractive girl. As soon as Joe was sure of the three hundred dollars she'd come back here and get what they all had to have — and somehow squeeze out the few pennies for dress material and the hair ribbon.

She stood here thinking of these things and so many others — a tall and rather comely woman in her early thirties, dark-faced and carrying an even, sweet-lipped gravity while her eyes sought the dry-goods shelves and her hand unconsciously patted the baby's round middle.

A woman came bustling into the store and said in a loud, accented voice: "Why, Hester Blount, of all the people I never expected to see!"

Hester said, "Now, isn't this a surprise!" and the two took each other's hands, and fell into a quick half embrace. Ten years ago they had been girls together over in the Two Dance, Hester and this Lila Evenson who had married a town man. Lila was turning into a heavy woman and, like many heavy women, she loved white and wore it now, though it made her look big as a house. Above the tight collar of the dress, her skin was a flushed red and a second chin faintly trembled when she talked. Hester Blount stood motionless, listening to that outpour of words, feeling the quick search of Lila's eyes. Lila, she knew, would be taking everything in — her worn dress, her heavy shoes, and the lines of her face.

"And another baby!" said Lila and bent over it and made a long gurgling sound. "What a lucky woman! That's three? But ain't it a problem, out there on Christmas Creek? Even in town here I worry so much over my one darling."

"No," said Hester, "we don't worry. How is your husband?"

"So well," said Lila. "You know, he's bought the drugstore from old Kerrin, who is getting old. He had done so well. We are lucky, as we keep telling ourselves. And that reminds me. You must come up to dinner. You really must come this minute."

They had been brought up on adjoining ranches and had ridden to the same school and to the same dances. But that was so long ago, and so much had changed them. And Lila was always a girl to throw her fortunes in other people's faces. Hester said, gently, regretfully: "Now, isn't it too bad! We brought a big lunch in the wagon, thinking it would be easier. Joe has so many chores to do here."

"I have often wondered about you, away out there," said Lila. "Have you been well? It's been such a hard year for everybody. So many homesteaders going broke."

"We are well," said Hester slowly, a small, hard pride in her tone. "Everything's been fine."

"Now, that's nice," murmured Lila, her smile remaining fixed; but her eyes, Hester observed, were sharp and busy — and reading too much. Lila said, "Next time you come and see us," and bobbed her head and went out of the store, her clothes rustling in this quiet. Hester's lips went sharp-shut and quick color burned on her cheeks. She took up the baby and turned into the street again and saw that Tom hadn't come yet to the wagon. The children were out of sight and there was nothing to do but wait. Hearing the far-off halloo of a train's whistle, she walked on under the board galleries to the depot.

Heat swirled around her and light flashed up from polished spots on the iron rails. Around her lay the full monotony of the desert, so familiar, so wide — and sometimes so hard to bear. Backed against the yellow depot wall, she watched the train rush forward, a high plume of white steam rising to the sky as it whistled to warn them. And then it rushed by, engine and cars, in a great smash of sound that stirred the baby in her arms. She saw men standing on the platforms. Women's faces showed in the car windows, serene and idly curious and not a part of Hester's world at all; and afterward the train was gone, leaving behind the heated smell of steel and smoke. When the quiet came back it was lonelier than before. She turned back to the wagon.

It was then almost twelve. The children

came up, hot and weary and full of excitement. Young Tom said: "The school is right in town. They don't have to walk at all. It's right next to the houses. Why don't they have to walk three miles like us?" And May said: "I saw a china doll with real clothes and painted eyelashes. Can I have a china doll?"

Hester changed the baby on the wagon seat. She said: "Walking is good for people, Tom. Why should you expect a doll now, May? Christmas is the time. Maybe Christmas we'll remember."

"Well, I'm hungry."

"Wait till your father comes," said Hester.

When he turned in from the street, later, she knew something was wrong. He was always a deliberate man, not much given to smiling. But he walked with his shoulders down and when he came up he said only: "I suppose we ought to eat." He didn't look directly at her. He had his own strong pride and she knew this wasn't like him — to stand by the wagon's wheel, so oddly watching his children. She reached under the seat for the box of sandwiches and the cups and the jug of cold coffee. She said: "What did he say, Joe?"

"Why, nothing yet. He said come back at two. He wanted to think about it."

She murmured, "It won't hurt us to wait," and laid out the sandwiches. They sat on the shaded ground and ate, the children with a quick, starved impatience, with an excited and aimless talk. Joe Blount looked at them carefully. "What was it you saw in the restaurant, sonny?"

"It smelled nice," said young May. "The smell came out the door."

Joe Blount cleared his throat. "Don't stop like that in front of the restaurant again."

"Can we go now? Can we go down by the depot?"

"You hold May's hand," said Blount, and watched them leave. He sat cross-legged before his wife, his big hands idle, his expression unstirred. The sandwich, which was salted bacon grease spread on Hester's potato bread lay before him. "Ain't done enough this morning to be hungry," he said.

"I know."

They were never much at talking. And now there wasn't much to say. She knew that he had been turned down. She knew that at two o'clock he would go and come back empty-handed. Until then she wouldn't speak of it, and neither would he. And she was thinking with a woman's realism of what lay before them. They had nothing except this team and wagon and two cows standing unfed in the barn lot. Going back to Christmas Creek now would be going back only to pack up and leave. For they had delayed asking for this loan until the last sack of flour in the storehouse had been emptied.

He said: "I been thinking. Not much to do on the ranch this fall. I ought to get a little outside work."

"Maybe you should."

"Fact is, I've tried a few places. Kind of quiet. But I can look around some more."

She said, "I'll wait here."

He got up, a rangy, spare man who found it hard to be idle. He looked at her carefully and his voice didn't reveal anything: "If I were you I don't believe I'd order anything at the stores until I come back."

She watched the way he looked out into the smoky horizon, the way he held his shoulders. When he turned away, not meeting her eyes, her lips made a sweet line across her dark face, a softly maternal expression showing. She said, "Joe," and waited until he turned. "Joe, we'll always get along."

He went away again, around the corner of the Cattle King. She shifted her position on the wagon's seat, her hand gently patting the baby who was a little cross from the heat.

One by one she went over the list of necessary things in her mind, and one by one, erased them. It was hard to think of little May without a ribbon in her hair, without a good dress. Boys could wear old clothes, as long as they were warm; but a girl, a pretty girl, needed the touch of niceness. It was hard to be poor.

Coming out of the bank at noon, Lane McKercher looked into the corral space and saw the Blounts eating their lunch under the locust tree. He turned down Arapahoe Street, walking through the comforting shade of the poplars to the big square house at the end of the lane. At dinner hour his boy took care of the bank, and so he ate his meal with the housekeeper in a dining room whose shades had been tightly drawn — the heavy midday meal of a man who had developed his hunger and his physique from early days on the range. Afterward he walked to the living-room couch and lay down with a paper over his face for the customary nap.

A single fly made a racket in the deep quiet, but it was not this that kept him from sleeping. In some obscure manner the shape of Joe Blount came before him — the long, patient and work-stiffened shape of a man whose eyes had been so blue and so calm in face of refusal. Well, there had been something behind those eyes for a moment, and then it had passed away, eluding McKercher's sharp glance.

They were mostly all patient ones and seldom speaking — these men that came off the deep desert. A hard life had made them that way, as McKercher knew, who had shared that life himself. Blount was no different than the others and many times McKercher had refused these others, without afterthoughts. It was some other thing that kept his mind on Blount. Not knowing why, he lay quietly on the couch, trying to find the reason.

The country, he told himself, was cattle country, and those who tried to dry-farm it were bound to fail. He had seen them fail, year after year. They took their wagons and their families out toward Christmas Creek, loaded high with plunder; and presently they came back with their wagons baked and their eyebrows bleached and nothing left. With their wives sitting in the wagons, old from work, with their children long and thin from lack of food. They had always failed and always would. Blount was a good man, but so were most of the rest. Why should he be thinking of Blount?

He rose at one o'clock, feeling the heat and feeling his age; and washed his hands and face with good cold water. Lighting a cigar, he strolled back down Arapahoe and walked across the square toward the Cattle King. Mrs. Blount sat on the wagon's seat, holding a baby: The older youngsters, he noticed, were in the cool runway of Dunmire's stable. He went into the saloon, though not to drink.

"Nick," he said, "Joe Blount been in for a drink yet?"

The saloonkeeper looked up from an empty poker table. "No," he said.

McKercher went out, crossing to Billy Saxton's feed store. Deep in the big shed Billy Saxton weighed hay bales on his heavy scales. He stopped and sopped the sweat off his forehead, and smiled. "Bankin'," he stated, "is easier."

"Maybe it is," said Lane McKercher. "You know Joe Blount well?"

"Why, he's all right. Used to ride for Hat. Old man Dale liked him. He was in here a while back."

"To buy feed?"

"No, he wanted to haul wood for me."

McKercher went back up the street toward the bank. Jim Benbow was coming down the road from the Two Dance hills, kicking a long streamer of dust behind. Sun struck the windows on the north side of town, setting up a brilliant explosion of light. Joe Blount came out of the stable and turned over toward the Cattle King, waiting for Benbow.

In the bank, McKercher said to his son, "All right, you go eat," and sat down at his pine desk. Benbow put his head through the front door calling: "I'll need five thousand this week, Mac — until the stock check comes in."

"All right."

He sat quite still at the desk, stern with himself because he could not recall why he kept thinking of Joe Blount. Men were everything to Lane McKercher, who watched them pass along this street year in and year out, who studied them with his sharp eyes and made his judgments concerning them. If there was something in a man, it had to come out. And what was it in Joe Blount he couldn't name? The echoes of the big clock on the wall rattled around the droning silence of the bank like the echo of feet striking the floor; it was then a quarter of two, and he knew he had to refuse Blount a second time. He could not understand why he had not made the first turndown final.

Blount met Jim Benbow on the corner of the Cattle King, directly after Hat's owner had left the bank. He shook Benbow's hand, warmed and pleased by the tall cattleman's smile of recognition. Benbow said: "Been a long time since I saw you. How's Christmas Creek, Joe?"

"Fine — just fine. You're lookin' good. You don't get old."

"Well, let's go have a little smile on that."

"Why, thanks, no. I was wonderin'. It's pretty quiet on my place right now. Not much to do till spring. You need a man?"

Benbow shook his head. "Not a thing doing, Joe. Sorry."

"Of course — of course," murmured Blount. "I didn't figure there would be."

He stood against the Cattle King's low porch rail after Benbow had gone down the street, his glance lifted and fixed on the smoky light of the desert beyond town. Shade lay around him but sweat began to creep below his hatbrim. He was closely and quickly thinking of places that might be open for a man, and knew there were none in town and none on the range. This was the slack season of the year. The children were over in front of the grocery store, stopped by its door, hand in hand, round, dark cheeks lifted and still. Blount swung his shoulders around, cutting them out of his sight.

Sullen Ben Drury came out of the courthouse and passed Blount, removing his cigar and speaking, and replacing the cigar again. Its smell was like acid biting at Blount's jaw corners, and suddenly he faced the bank with the odd and terrible despair of a man who has reached the end of hope, and a strange thought came to him, which was that the doors of that bank were wide open and money lay on the counter inside for the taking.

He stood very still, his head down, and after a while he thought: "An unseemly thing for a man to hold in his head." It was two o'clock then and he turned over the square, going toward the bank with his legs springing as he walked and all his muscles loose. In the quietness of the room his boots dragged up odd sound. He stood by Lane McKercher's desk, waiting without any show of expression; he knew what McKercher would say.

McKercher said, slowly and with an odd trace of irritation: "Joe, you're wasting your time on Christmas Creek. And you'd waste the loan."

Blount said, mildly and courteously: "I

255

can understand your view. Don't blame you for not loanin' without security." He looked over McKercher's head, his glance going through the window to the far strip of horizon. "Kind of difficult to give up a thing," he mused. "I figured to get away from ridin' for other folks and ride for myself. Well, that was why we went to Christmas Creek. Maybe a place the kids could have later. Man wants his children to have somethin' better than he had."

"Not on Christmas Creek," said McKercher. He watched Joe Blount with a closer and sharper interest, bothered by a feeling he could not name. Bothered by it and turned impatient by it.

"Maybe, maybe not," said Blount. "Bad luck don't last forever." Then he said, "Well, I shouldn't be talkin'. I thank you for your time." He put on his hat, and his big hand moved up across his shirt, to the pocket there — and dropped away. He turned toward the door.

"Hold on," said Lane. "Hold on a minute." He waited till Blount came back to the desk. He opened the desk's drawer and pulled out a can of cigars, holding them up. "Smoke?"

There was a long delay, and it was strange to see the way Joe Blount looked at the cigars, with his lips closely together. He said, his voice dragging on the words, "I guess not, but thanks."

Lane McKercher looked down at the desk, his expression breaking out of its maintained strictness. The things in a man had to come out, and he knew now why Joe Blount had stayed so long in his mind. It made him look up. "I have been considering this. It won't ever be a matter of luck on Christmas Creek. It's a matter of water. When I passed the feed store today I noticed a second hand windmill in the back. It will do. You get hold of Plummer Bodry and find out his price for driving you a well. I never stake a man unless I stake him right. We will figure the three hundred and whatever it takes to put up a tank and windmill. When you buy your supplies today, just say you've got credit here."

"Why, now —" began Joe Blount in his slow, soft voice, "I —"

But Lane McKercher said to his son, just coming back from lunch, "I want you to bring your ledger over here." He kept on talking and Joe Blount, feeling himself pushed out, turned and left the bank.

McKercher's son came over. "Made that loan after all. Why?"

McKercher said only, "He's a good man, Bob." But he knew the real reason. A man that smoked always carried his tobacco in his shirt pocket. Blount had kept reaching, out of habit, for something that wasn't there. Well, a man like Blount loved this one small comfort and never went without it unless actually destitute. But Blount wouldn't admit it, and had been too proud to take a free cigar. Men were everything — and the qualities in them came out sooner or later, as with Blount. A windmill and water was a good risk with a fellow like that.

Hester watched him cross the square and come toward her, walking slowly, with his shoulders squared. She patted the baby's back and gently rocked it, and wondered at the change. When he came up he said, casually, "I'll hitch and drive around to the store, so we can load the stuff you buy."

She watched him carefully, so curious to know how it had happened. But she only said: "We'll get along."

He was smiling then, he who seldom smiled. "I guess you need a few things for yourself. We can spare something for that."

"Only a dress and some ribbon, for May. A girl needs something nice." She paused, and afterward added, because she knew how real his need was, "Joe, you buy yourself some tobacco."

He let out a long, long breath. "I believe

I will," he said. They stood this way, both gently smiling. They needed no talk to explain anything to each other. They had been through so much these last few years. Hardship and trouble had drawn them so close together that words were unnecessary. So they were silent, remembering so much, and understanding so much, and still smiling. Presently he turned to hitch up.

Ernest Haycox during his lifetime was considered the dean among authors of Western fiction. When the Western Writers of America was first organized in 1953, what became the Golden Spur Award for outstanding achievement in writing Western fiction was first going to be called the "Erny" in homage to Haycox. He was born in Portland, Oregon and, while still an undergraduate at the University of Oregon in Eugene, sold his first short story to the OVERLAND MONTHLY. His name soon became established in all the leading pulp magazines of the day, including Street and Smith's WESTERN STORY MAGAZINE and Doubleday's WEST MAGAZINE. His first novel, FREE GRASS, was published in book form in 1929. In 1931 he broke into the pages of COLLIER'S and from that time on was regularly featured in this magazine, either with a short story or a serial that was later published as a novel. In the 1940s his serials began appearing in THE SATURDAY EVENING POST and it was there that modern classics such as BUGLES IN THE AFTERNOON (1944) and CANYON PASSAGE (1945) were first published. Both of these novels were also made into major motion pictures although, perhaps, the film most loved and remembered is STAGECOACH (United Artists, 1939) directed by John Ford and starring John Wayne, based on Haycox's short story "Stage to Lordsburg." No history of the Western story in the 20th Century would be possible without references to Haycox's fiction and his tremendous influence on other writers of stature, such as Peter Dawson, Norman A. Fox, Wayne D. Overholser, and Luke Short, among many. During his last years, before his premature death from abdominal carcinoma, he set himself the task of writing historical fiction which he felt would provide a fitting legacy and the consummation of his life's work. He almost always has an involving story to tell and one in which there is something not so readily definable that raises it above its time, an image possibly, a turn of phrase, or even a sensation, the smell of dust after rain or the solitude of an Arizona night. Haycox was an author whose Western fiction has made an abiding contribution to world literature.

We hope you have enjoyed this Large Print book. Other Thorndike Press or Chivers Press Large Print books are available at your library or directly from the publishers.

For more information about current and upcoming titles, please call or write, without obligation, to:

Thorndike Press
P.O. Box 159
Thorndike, Maine 04986 USA
Tel. (800) 223-2336

OR

Chivers Press Limited
Windsor Bridge Road
Bath BA2 3AX
England
Tel. (0225) 335336

All our Large Print titles are designed for easy reading, and all our books are made to last.